Five minutes and counting...

And then the bombs would explode the vessel.

They couldn't swim away fast enough or far enough, but maybe they could dive and be safe beneath the surface.

Fear rushed through Kirk, and fire surged through his legs as he ran to Cora's cabin. She might be asleep, recovering from her earlier fight with death.

He burst through the door. "We have less than four minutes to gear up in scuba and get off this ship. Or we're going to die." He ushered her into the hallway.

She stopped. "What about the others?"

"I can't save them. But I can save you." Maybe. "Now get geared up. We might already be too late."

Dive suits. Mask, regulator, tanks, flippers. He worked as fast as he could.

Before they could hit the water, the crack of an explosion resounded and the deck shifted beneath them.

Elizabeth Goddard is the award-winning author of more than thirty novels and novellas. A 2011 Carol Award winner, she was a double finalist in the 2016 Daphne du Maurier Award for Excellence in Mystery/Suspense, and a 2016 Carol Award finalist. Elizabeth graduated with a computer science degree and worked in high-level software sales before retiring to write full-time.

Books by Elizabeth Goddard

Love Inspired Suspense

Coldwater Bay Intrigue

Thread of Revenge
Stormy Haven
Distress Signal

Texas Ranger Holidays

Texas Christmas Defender

Wilderness, Inc.

Targeted for Murder
Undercover Protector
False Security
Wilderness Reunion

Mountain Cove

Buried
Untraceable
Backfire
Submerged
Tailspin
Deception

Visit the Author Profile page at Harlequin.com for more titles.

DISTRESS SIGNAL

ELIZABETH
GODDARD

⟨H⟩ **HARLEQUIN**® LOVE INSPIRED® SUSPENSE

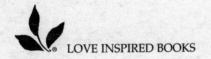 LOVE INSPIRED BOOKS

ISBN-13: 978-1-335-23184-0

Distress Signal

www.Harlequin.com

Printed in U.S.A.

Who shall separate us from the love of Christ?
shall tribulation, or distress, or persecution,
or famine, or nakedness, or peril, or sword?
—Romans 8:35

Dedicated to my youngest, Andrew.
If God is for us, who can be against us?

It's with heartfelt gratitude that I say THANK YOU to
an amazing editor I've had the privilege of working with
at Love Inspired Suspense for years—Elizabeth Mazer.
Thank you for believing in me and my stories!

ONE

This wasn't the way she wanted to die.

Every muscle screaming, Cora Strand swam toward the shore through a viscous, muddy swamp. Oily blackness and green slime clung to her whole body, and it felt like a slow suffocation. But no matter what she did, she couldn't seem to make it to the distant, gray, mist-shrouded beach. As if that wasn't bad enough, the more she swam, the deeper she sank. The swamp, like lique-fied quicksand, sucked her under, inch by inch.

Through all her swimming, all her efforts, she repeated these words: "It's only a dream. Only a dream. Only a nightmare."

Muscles ached. Lungs burned. She swam faster and harder but she couldn't escape the gooey gunk that pulled her down, down, down. Tugged her deeper into the abyss.

She couldn't afford to let it pull her completely under because then it would be game over. She knew without a doubt she wouldn't resurface, even as some part of her psyche told her it was a dream.

She had to escape the darkness.

Just stop fighting. Just...let go... Something inside

of her whispered the words and she was tempted to listen. If she stopped fighting, and sank into it, then she would be at peace forever.

"Cora." The smooth masculine voice was only vaguely familiar to her.

And with the voice, that same fear strangled her. Death seemed to reach for her from the swamp.

Cora sucked in a sharp breath.

Open. Open my eyes...

Her lashes fluttered as she forced her lids slowly up.

Deep, piercing blue eyes stared at her. She knew those eyes—that gaze didn't miss a thing.

Kirk Higgins. The broad-chested diver. Sun-bleached curls hung to his shoulders, and his square, tanned jaw worked back and forth as concern lined his forehead. This guy looked nothing like his brother, Stephan—the man she'd almost fallen for once upon a time. Stephan had been a liar. Still, she'd lied to herself first, telling herself that she wanted Stephan in the first place.

It had always been Kirk.

His presence here on the Research Vessel *Sea Dragon* reminded her of that broken part of her heart on a daily basis. After all, he'd been the one to introduce her to Stephan.

Kirk's pupils dilated as he caught his breath. "You're awake. Cora? Do you know who I am?"

If only he knew what she'd been thinking. Unable to form words yet, she nodded, then finally said, "You're Ste— Er... Kirk."

His tenuous smile told her he was genuinely worried. "That's right. I'm Kirk, not my brother, Stephan."

Her mouth dry, she smacked her lips. "What happened?"

He frowned. "I was hoping you could tell me."

The fear and sense of imminent death followed her from the dream. Cora tried to sit up on her elbows and failed. Where was she? She looked around, expecting a hospital, perhaps. But it was only her stateroom on the *Sea Dragon*, the research vessel used by the marine archaeological group with which she worked. A new job. A dream come true. Now all turned wrong. She sensed that, anyway, but didn't know why. Couldn't fully comprehend it.

She reached up and ran her hand through her hair. With the action she noted the IV in her arm connected to a saline bag. "I don't know what happened. Just tell me why I'm waking up in my room to find you staring at me. We could start with that."

"We almost lost you." Thick emotion edged his voice.

A flash of something—bubbles accosting her beneath the surface. "I was swimming."

He nodded as if urging her to continue.

"Diving with the team for a shipwreck?"

"No. We're field-testing the ROV, remember? But there was a problem. We ordered a part and have been waiting."

Of course, she remembered that part. The ROV— remotely-operated underwater vehicle. Lance Maier, the ROV operator, called it Trigon, after a villain from a comic book, because he constantly had trouble with it.

"Most of the crew took off while we wait. Paula and Brian headed to Seattle for a few days."

Paula Timber and Brian Holland—other than Cora, they were the only members of the science team.

They'd been operating with a small crew—just twenty people, including the support crew, deckhands, engineers, electricians—everyone needed to operate the research vessel as they supported the small science crew.

Still, how had she ended up like this? "I don't understand. What happened?"

His lips flattened. He got up and grabbed a mug from the counter. "Here, drink this."

She sat up on her elbows, successfully this time, the itchy sheets digging into her skin. The movement caused multiple hammers to beat her skull. It was then she noticed that he'd kept the lights low. Squinting her eyes, she peered down at the mug. "What is it?"

"Water." Arms crossed, he remained standing there like a sentinel watching over her as he studied her. A million questions seemed to pulse behind his gaze.

If she tried, she could almost forget he was Stephan's brother. But maybe she should remember the kind of man Stephan turned out to be. Kirk could well be a liar, too. She would stick to the plan she'd made when, to her absolute shock, the man had joined the *Sea Dragon*.

He thrust the mug at her again. This time she took it and drank like she'd been drifting on a raft too long at sea. The cool liquid eased down her parched throat and tasted so good.

"You went missing. Disappeared down there. At least, that's what Trip and Coburn claim. They searched until they had to return."

Trip Dahmer, in charge of communications, and Declan Coburn—maritime security. At least she could remember names and faces.

Cora let the water roll around in her mouth before she swallowed against the lump that had grown thick in her throat.

I went missing?

If she'd been diving and something happened so that she was left out there, she would have run out of oxygen, too. She read the truth of that in Kirk's eyes. What had happened? How had she gotten lost? Visibility had oftentimes been an issue due to murky river runoff that created silty conditions, but they had good visibility in this location. Still, she was working off a faulty memory.

More importantly… "Who found me?"

Kirk slowly eased into the chair next to her bed, giving her the impression that he'd held an all-night vigil on her behalf. "I did."

She'd been stunned when he'd been hired two months ago to work aboard the research vessel where she'd landed a job as a shipwreck archaeologist. Apparently he'd been someone with the kind of diving experience they needed after their most knowledgeable diver had been arrested on drug charges, which had come as a surprise to all of them, considering his credentials.

But Kirk also had his own impressive list of archaeological credentials to go along with his notable diving skills and jack-of-all-trades knowledge about how to fix everything. He'd been in the navy, too. A perfect fit for the job. Just not the perfect fit for working with her. But Cora had kept her mouth shut. She didn't want anyone to know her past with his brother and wouldn't let that get in the way of teamwork or professionalism. Besides, it had been years.

They were different people now. She'd let the past stay there. And it wasn't the past that worried her now. More like the future.

Unfortunately, she was still as fascinated with him

as she'd been when they'd met years ago, which unnerved her. She couldn't exactly put her finger on the reason why she was drawn to Kirk. She only knew that she had to steer clear of him.

Suddenly aware of his rapt attention as he waited for her to keep drinking, she sipped from the cup and watched him over the rim.

"The crew is bringing the medic back with them from Farrow Island. Shari told us not to move you more than I already did when I brought you here," he said.

They were part of a medical advisory service that could communicate with doctors twenty hours per day via ship-to-shore communications if needed when in remote areas. But this wasn't that remote. The research vessel had anchored in the Salish Sea, several nautical miles from Farrow Island in the Rosario Strait off the coast of Washington. The island was part of the San Juan Islands and filled with tourists.

Kirk continued. "He assured us that you probably bumped your head and that you would wake up soon."

From the way he frowned, the look in his eyes, she got the feeling that he hadn't been so sure. Cora had the distinct feeling that something was going on here, but she kept her suspicions to herself.

Maybe Kirk did, too. An emotion she couldn't define lurked in his gaze and it sent a chill over her. She recognized that look as one she'd seen before in Stephan's eyes and knew all too well. What was he hiding?

As if sensing her unease, he got up, poured more water from a pitcher and handed it to her. "Drink."

She refused. "I'm good. Thank you…thank you for finding me. For saving me."

"Do you remember anything about what happened?" he asked.

She shook her head and rested back on the pillow. Her memory was all a blank slate. A black hole. "Considering the dream I just had, I'm going to guess I was pretty far gone."

He looked at her, seeing right through her, it seemed. He said nothing in response to her declaration, but that was just as well. Hearing the words out loud might bring the dream to life, and she definitely wanted it to stay dead.

If she had been…gone…he likely had given her CPR. Though it was a lifesaving technique, she imagined his lips pressed to hers, blowing breath into her body. Reviving her.

She wouldn't ask him about that part. Not yet, at least.

"What was your dream about? Maybe it's somehow connected to what happened to you out there."

You would have to ask. "You know how dreams are. I can't really describe it other than it left me with the impression I was dying. Darkness was pulling me under."

He squeezed her hand. Reassuring her? For some strange reason, Kirk's touch on her hand made her feel even more off-kilter. Especially since she didn't think she had as much as brushed shoulders with him in all the time they'd been working together. It had seemed he tried to avoid her as much as she avoided him, though that proved difficult at times.

Back in her college days—after everything that had happened involving Stephan and, yes, Kirk—she'd vowed never to get involved again. At least, not enough to actually fall for someone. Fortunately her career, keeping her dream alive, had kept her too occupied to consider a relationship…that was, until Kirk showed up. And that annoyed her to no end.

Averting her gaze, she bit her lip. Hard. She had much worse problems than Kirk. What was she supposed to do with a memory wipe? Well, at least it wasn't a complete wipe.

A new kind of fear coursed through her. Was it possible she could lose her research job here on the *Sea Dragon* where she confirmed and documented reports of shipwrecks?

Cora didn't like that. Not one bit. She'd better get her act together and fast. She couldn't let that happen. She'd worked too hard to get here. This job was what helped her measure up to her amazingly successful siblings. Sadie was a marine biologist who traveled the world in her research, though her traveling had slowed down since she'd married Gage Sessions, who was with the Coast Guard Investigative Services. Then there was Jonna, who'd been a special agent with the Homeland Security Investigations division of ICE—Immigration and Customs Enforcement—and traded that in to run her own inn as well as working alongside her private investigator security specialist husband, Ian Brady. And, finally, Quinn, who was always working deep undercover with the DEA—Drug Enforcement Administration.

No. She simply couldn't afford this kind of setback.

Kirk shifted closer, reminding her that he was here, watching her. How on earth could she have forgotten?

"I'm just glad you're awake now, and looks like you're no worse for the wear."

"Except I can't remember what happened." She

blurted that out with entirely too much emotion. Considering the state she'd woken up in, it was definitely worth remembering.

Kirk tilted his head. "That's not out of the ordinary. People often forget exactly what happened during, say, a car wreck or other traumatic event—it's called retrograde amnesia. The memories will likely come back to you, though you might wish they hadn't."

I know all that. I'm a scientist, remember? She kept that to herself. She appreciated his reassurance, really, but… "What are you now, a therapist?"

His chuckle was confident and robust. She liked the sound of it, which was truly unfortunate. She didn't want to like even one more thing about this man.

"I'm just a friend who is going to let you rest while I go find out what is holding up the crew and Shari. Plus, the part for the ROV finally came in today. Trip went with them to the island to gather supplies and pick up the part. It's just you, me, Captain Menken and Lance aboard."

"Well, call Shari and tell her that she doesn't have to rush back. I'm fine. I'm awake. She can enjoy the time on land."

He shook his head. "I think she should take a look, and if you're okay, then, sure, she can go back. It will take Lance time to fix the ROV, even with the part in hand. But Shari could suggest you get an MRI, in which case we'll have to transport you to Seattle. Let's get you checked out just to be sure." Despite the positive lilt to his voice, worry lingered in his deep blue gaze.

Return to Seattle for an MRI. All because of something that had happened to her while diving—some mistake she'd made, perhaps. Yep. She could very well lose her job. "I need to get back to work. I can't afford to lie around. I'm fine, Kirk. Really. I feel great." An exaggeration, maybe, but she had to be convincing. She shook off the chill that just wouldn't leave her. A chill that went beyond the physical.

"Come on, Cora. It's me, remember? And I don't care what you say—you're not fine until Shari *says* you're fine. You stay there and rest until she can give you a once over. I started an IV. Got you hydrated."

He'd done much more than that—he'd saved her life.

"Fine," she huffed. "I'll stay put...for now."

Kirk flicked off the lights in her small quarters as he stood at the door, the silhouette of his broad shoulders and lean physique filling the doorway.

"Would you mind leaving those on?" Her stateroom didn't have a porthole, so no light could come in from outside.

"Sure." He turned the lights back on. Just before he closed the door, he leaned back in and said, "Lock the door behind me." He touched the bolt. "Use the dead bolt."

He grinned as if his request wasn't any big deal. Except, the way he said the words, it was almost as if he knew exactly what had happened to her. The tone in his voice tugged a shadow from her dream that descended on her. Her complete paranoia seemed ridiculous and yet...*not*. Cora tried to rest but too much bothered her. She popped a couple of ibuprofen tablets. A few minutes later, she felt good enough to walk the passageways and maybe jar the memories back into place. Kirk wouldn't be happy, but he wasn't her boss, though it made her feel good that he was so protective and concerned.

Still, despite what she'd promised, she couldn't stay in bed.

And, besides, she was fine. She was going to be all right. Cora would keep telling herself that and maybe it would be true.

The memories will likely come back to you, though you might wish they hadn't.

One thing she *did* remember was that they had received new information about a possible shipwreck. And that excited her.

Scientists believed that approximately three million ships could be found at the bottom of the ocean. To date, only about ten percent had ever been found. Of course, treasure hunters searched for the cargo held by those ships, but Cora wasn't that kind of treasure hunter. Her treasure was history. She was an archaeologist and a historian. She used satellite imagery, ocean mapping and other technologies to find and confirm the shipwrecks, and would then dive, if possible, to see for herself and document what she found.

The thought of finding another shipwreck got her mind off other worrisome matters, and she needed that. Galvanized, she decided to work at the computer in the lab to look at the coordinates.

Kirk and Captain Menken would likely scold her for not resting. Lance would definitely be furious. He had a thing for her, she could tell, but she hadn't encouraged him in that. Maybe she would have eventually, but then Kirk had shown up.

Whatever. She couldn't stand being alone in her room. Not with the remnants of that dream still haunting her mind.

It didn't help that this big boat was eerily quiet, but

she reminded herself that when the crew went ashore it was partially a ghost ship.

A door creaked and Cora froze. She'd thought most everyone had gone to the island, as Kirk had said. She peered around the corner. The man himself stepped out of Trip's quarters. Her pulse jumped.

What was he doing in there? Trip had gone to the island, right? That's what Kirk had said earlier. She waited until he moved out of sight, hoping and praying panic wouldn't set in. There had to be an explanation.

Maybe Trip had communicated from the island and needed Kirk to check something for him. She wouldn't jump to conclusions.

As Cora made her way to the hydrographic lab, she tried to tamp down the rising unease. Opening the door, she flicked on the lights and stepped inside. She wouldn't ask about Kirk's reason for being in Trip's room. No, instead, she'd let Trip know. Either Kirk had business in there or he didn't, but Trip could decide how to handle it.

She booted up the computer. Goose bumps crawled over her arms as she slowly turned her head.

Trip.

His body.

He lay in a pool of blood.

With a deep stab wound to his chest.

Cora screamed but couldn't hear the sound. Panic-stricken, she ran from the room. She had to get hold of herself and call for help.

Captain…Captain Menken.

She had to find the man and report a…a…murder! Her trembling limbs couldn't carry her if she didn't suck it up. She had to be strong. For Trip's sake and for her own safety.

Kirk. He'd just come from Trip's room. He'd said Trip had gone ashore, but no, Trip was dead. Murdered. She was on board the *Sea Dragon* with a murderer.

From the dark oppression of her dream, an impression, more than a memory, rose up inside with tendrils of fear that slithered around her. And, suddenly, she knew without a doubt that someone had tried to kill her, but they had succeeded in murdering Trip instead.

Time was running out.

Pulse spiking, Kirk steadied his breath as he crept down the hall. He needed to communicate with his superior, Matt Patterson, about his discovery. He wasn't entirely sure it meant anything, but he had a hunch it could mean everything.

Working NCIS undercover—Naval Criminal Investigative Service—Kirk's methods for obtaining that information hadn't exactly been on the up-and-up. He wouldn't tell them that yet, though. He shouldn't have gone into Trip's room without his permission. Nor should he have hacked into his laptop. The guy had been acting strangely, setting off warning signals in Kirk's head. Time to dig deeper.

He'd justified his decision to break protocol in this undercover operation with the fact that someone had obviously tried to kill Cora. Kirk hadn't let on just how terrified he was for her. He hadn't told her that her regulator hose had been cut. She didn't seem to remember what happened, which was just as well for the time being. As long as she stayed locked in her room, she'd be safe for now. All the likely guilty parties had gone ashore.

So he'd slipped into Trip's room to get some answers before it was too late. Kirk's time to find those answers was almost up. With the attack on Cora, a murderer's clock had begun counting down, and fast.

Kirk had become desperate—a position in which he never wanted to find himself. Given the circumstances, he'd grabbed his Glock and carried it on his person.

He was glad for the skeleton crew currently on the research vessel. Quietly entering the passageway that would take him to the helm, he thought back to the moment he'd found her. His chest constricted. She'd been fortunate to survive. In fact, he wasn't sure how he'd found or revived her. God must have been watching over her.

Kirk found her washed up on a nearby sandbar and had given her CPR. Without knowing how long she'd been under, he hadn't even been sure he could revive her.

But this was Cora! He'd sent up frantic prayers as he battled for her life. He should have done more to protect her. Then she'd coughed up water.

He almost couldn't believe it.

Her lids had fluttered open. Sheer terror had coursed through him—what would he see in her eyes? A tsunami of relief washed over him at the recognition in her gaze.

She'd mumbled something, then her eyes closed again. He couldn't wake her. The fear rushed back.

Kirk had then swum her to the *Sea Dragon* where he'd remained in the room with her until all suspicious parties had gone to Farrow Island.

As far as Kirk was concerned, Trip and Coburn were both responsible. They had lost her. Left her down there. And maybe even cut her hose. They claimed she'd speared a shark and somehow gotten tangled and it had taken off with her. He'd torn into them as much as he could without coming to actual blows. The captain had been forced to come between them, and he'd sent them to get the medic, Shari, and pick up the ROV part and supplies.

Hence the rules had to be bent. Kirk needed answers right now.

He'd been working on the *Sea Dragon* for two months already and should have learned something about what had happened to Drake Jackson—son of Navy Commander Brent Jackson. Drake had gone missing six months ago and was believed dead. Kirk had approached Brent Jackson directly about looking for Kirk's childhood best friend.

So far, Kirk hadn't made any progress on that front, but maybe what he'd discovered on Trip's computer was connected. He could envision Drake coming across sensitive information and losing his life for it.

That's why he'd been gutted when he learned Cora Strand was working with the crew of the *Sea Dragon*. Most everyone was likely aboveboard, but someone had nefarious intentions and Cora was much too close to danger. All the more reason for him to join the crew.

Years ago, he'd attended the University of Washington where he'd met Cora. They spent a lot of time together, but took their budding relationship slowly. Each of them had their own reasons for that. But they'd grown close, and he thought she could be someone he could have a future with. Then he introduced her to his conniving brother, and the rest was history. Stephan had worked his charm and whisked Cora away from Kirk before he'd even had a real chance with her.

Nothing new there. Kirk should have known it would happen. After all, Stephan had stolen his girlfriend when they were in high school. Why hadn't Kirk stopped him either time? Admittedly he had begun to get a complex.

Obviously, both women had preferred Stephan to Kirk. Now that he thought about it, introducing Cora to Stephan had been a test, of sorts. Might as well introduce her and see what happened before he got too romantically involved.

But Providence had a way of turning well-made plans upside down. The only woman he'd never been able to forget, a woman stolen by his brother, was here on the *Sea Dragon* and her life was in danger.

And Kirk could surmise that the same thing that had happened to Drake had almost happened to Cora today.

Thank You, God…that he'd been able to search for her and find her. His naval experience and diving skills had never come in handier.

With nothing but a bare-bones crew on board the research vessel today, this had been his best opportunity to search. The risk he'd taken had provided more information that might escalate this situation to a whole new level, if it hadn't been life-threatening enough.

He couldn't let Commander Jackson down.

Regardless, Kirk needed to wrap this up so no one else was killed and claimed to be missing. Namely Cora.

Kirk crept up to the helm to check on Captain Menken before he made the call to Matt. He needed to communicate what he'd learned and get further instructions before the gang returned from Farrow Island with Shari to check on Cora.

Stepping into the wheelhouse, he found it empty.

"Menken?" Where was the man?

Kirk swung his gaze around. Through the window, he caught sight of Captain Menken rowing away in a dinghy. They only had two—the others had taken the first one.

Kirk watched for a few seconds as his mind wrapped around this new development. Why was the captain leaving? Who was operating the research vessel? At least Menken could have asked Kirk about Cora before he took off.

Suspicion corded around his chest. What was going on? Kirk didn't like what he saw and his thoughts went straight to Cora. He should never have left her alone.

His gaze fell to red flashing numbers. *Counting down.*

An image blinked on a digital screen revealing several locations near the hull of the *Sea Dragon*.

His mind seized up as his heart stuttered.

Bombs.

He had to act. *Move, man!*

Letting his elite training kick in, he crouched to look at the bomb below the console—not the only one. Others were counting down, strategically placed to do the most damage.

To sink the research vessel and leave no survivors.

He wasn't sure he could defuse this one, but even if he could, he had no time to disarm the others.

He wasn't sure he even had time to get to Cora or find Lance before the *Sea Dragon* was blown to smithereens.

Ten minutes and counting. Adrenaline spiking, he set his diver's watch to count down with the bomb.

Those ten minutes would allow the captain to get to a safe distance.

Kirk got on the intercom and announced the emergency, hoping Lance and Cora would hear.

"Meet me at the stern immediately. The boat is about to blow!" He wished for another way to tell them the news, but there wasn't time. "Do not panic. Run for the stern. We have less than ten minutes to clear the vessel."

He escaped the helm and hurried to enact his plan.

Was it enough time to don diving gear? Being underwater during an explosion was the worst idea. It could kill them. Still, without another boat, he didn't think they could swim away fast enough or far enough. Even if they survived the blast, they couldn't survive the cold waters long enough to swim to the island. But maybe they could dive and get to a safe distance beneath the surface. Still, if they didn't get far enough away underwater, they could die that way, too. Not a lot of options. With each tick of the clock, their time was running out. At the moment, he wasn't sure he could even run fast enough. At the stern, he scrambled down the ladder to grab dive equipment and wet suits.

Fear rushed through him. "Cora! Lance! We're running out of time! Where are you?"

Captain Menken had left Lance, Cora and Kirk here to die. For certain, the captain had to be behind this. Fire surged through his legs as he ran to Cora's room. It was locked, which meant she had to be inside.

She might be asleep, recovering from her fight with death.

He banged on the door. "Cora, we have to get off this boat!"

"No. I'm staying right here."

"What are you talking about?" he demanded.

"You told me to lock the door, so it's locked. This is the safest place."

"Cora, there's a bomb. Didn't you hear my announcement?"

"No. I heard nothing."

Had communications been taken out? "I'm telling you, Cora, there's a bomb. Make that more than one. Many bombs. We have less than eight minutes to gear up and escape."

"Trip is dead."

"What are you talking about?" He didn't have time for this. "If you won't open the door, I'm coming in after you."

"To save me again?" What was with the sarcasm?

Kirk kicked at the door. The lock held. He was out of options here. "Move back. I'm shooting the lock out."

He followed through with his words, then kicked the door in. Cora stood in the corner holding her diver's knife. Terror filled her eyes.

"Do you plan to stab me with that?"

"Did you kill Trip?"

"What?" She wasn't making any sense. "Listen, both of us are going to die if we don't get off this boat." He disarmed her before she could put the knife to use on him, then ushered her out of the stateroom and down the hallway, despite her continued resistance.

"What about Lance? What about the captain?"

"The captain rowed away in a boat. If Lance got the

message he'll meet us at the stern. I have time to save you." Maybe.

Please, God...

Tears streamed down her face. "Did you kill him?"

Pain lashed through his heart. How could she even think that? "Of course not. We can hash this out later. Now get geared up. We might already be too late."

Dive suits. Masks, regulators, tanks, flippers. Buoyancy control vests. He'd never donned gear this fast.

He glanced at his diver's watch. Two minutes. Sweat poured down his face and back.

The other bombs might go off earlier, for all he knew.

As if to emphasize his thoughts, the crack of an explosion resounded. The deck shifted beneath them. Someone had gone to a lot of trouble to kill Cora.

To kill them both.

TWO

An unimaginable concussive force shoved Cora. Her legs and arms flew forward while her core took the brunt of the force, curving inward, as her body was tossed from the *Sea Dragon*.

Flying through the air as fire burst from the vessel beneath her, her mind had no time to think, no time to react or understand what was happening, except for one thing—the fear of imminent death grabbed her throat and choked the breath from her.

Oh, God, oh, God, oh, God... Please, help me!

She had no control over her life.

As the dark blue of the Salish Sea sped toward her, her arms and legs finally moved, grappling with the empty space—the air around her—as if she could grab on to something and break her fall. Her mind slowly began to catch up, to comprehend the events leading up to this moment.

A bomb had gone off somewhere—maybe near the hull at the bow of the vessel so the ship had absorbed much of the shockwave. Otherwise she might be unconscious or dead right now.

And with that knowledge—that she had survived

the explosion so far—she recognized and accepted the water, the fathomless sea coming toward her. The water she knew better than anything, and she knew that she could live through the cold of this sea shielded from the open and harsh waters of ocean by islands and the Olympic Peninsula. Had her scuba equipment, her tanks, been damaged by the explosion? *God, please let it not be so. Please help us!*

The water stopped her free fall through the air. She sank deep into the dark waters—but they weren't nearly as dark and angry as the wide-open northern Pacific Ocean, for which she couldn't have been more grateful.

She cleared her regulator then inserted it before heading for the surface, but a hand gripped hers and tugged her back. The flash of a memory, an image she couldn't wrap her mind around, sent cold fear through her. She almost fought him, then the shadow of the memory evaporated and Cora was back in the moment.

Kirk held her hand. Should she trust him? He'd been the one to blast his way into her room, disarm her and make sure she was ready to face what came next.

Not once had he hesitated in saving her when he could have saved himself and been long gone if he hadn't stayed behind for her.

The force of the blast alone could have killed her, but instead it had thrown her—thrown them both—from the vessel, shaking her world. Except Kirk was still here. He remained a rock.

Darkness loomed below as he tugged her deeper, swimming fast and furiously into the murky depths, to escape any additional blasts, despite the danger of descending too quickly. Above them the ocean rippled with bright flashes. Their greatest threat at the moment—debris.

Chunks of debris—large and small pieces—shot past them, cutting through the cloudy water and dropping like it was raining shards of what used to be the *Sea Dragon*.

A school of fish darted by in frantic escape.

Fueled by terror, her heart pounded. Not good. Cora tried to breathe steadily and evenly, the compressed air in her lungs a hazard all by itself. Before the blast, they had slipped on fins which allowed them to cut rapidly through the water. Except she'd lost one of them in the blast.

Despite her reservations about the man, she kept close to Kirk as he led the way, heading who knew where—their only goal to escape the vessel's untimely violent destruction.

Behind the mask, tears burned her eyes and her throat threatened to close up.

Focus. Breathe. Focus. Relax.

She let the bubbles rise around her and comfort her like they always did. And she prayed harder than she'd ever prayed before.

My life is threatened twice in one day, Lord? Please help me, help us escape. And please help me to know if I can trust this man.

Earlier in the day, she'd suspected Kirk of Trip's murder. But it could have been Lance, who'd also been on board. It could have been any one of the crew members. Someone could have killed him before they left for the island. The same someone who had tried to kill her.

And now, Lance… Had he died in the explosion? *Oh, Lance!* Her heart beat erratically to keep in rhythm with her crazy emotions. If only she could wipe her eyes.

She still breathed much too fast. *Oh, God, help me to calm down.* They'd survived this far; she didn't need to complicate their escape. She needed to focus on one thing at a time.

And right now, it was Kirk pulling her along as he put distance between them and the devastation.

She allowed that thought to comfort her as she remained near his side.

Where would he take them? His fast thinking in their escape—to don the diving equipment to be able to swim away from the blast faster, and to keep warm longer—had been a brilliant idea. He was protective, and for that she was grateful. She needed the reassurance of his strong, solid presence now, regardless of her suspicions and doubts.

It was just that after finding Trip's body she had no idea whom she could trust.

As if sensing her emotional and mental battles, Kirk angled his body toward her. Behind the mask, his grim expression twisted. He pointed up. She nodded that she understood he wanted to surface. They had to use hand signals because Kirk had grabbed the standard regulator valves so they couldn't use voice communications.

Of course, she was experienced and understood scuba hand signals perfectly.

But then what? Where would they go? Who could they trust? No. Make that who could *she* trust? Was it this man by her side? Yes, he'd saved her and if Kirk had truly wanted to kill her, he'd now had two opportunities. He could have left her for dead earlier in the day when she nearly drowned, or he could have left her on the boat to die.

Fine. She would trust him for the moment. But only

so far. She had to remain on guard until she was absolutely certain.

They slowly ascended to allow for decompression at the proper rate. Kirk kept an eye on his diver's watch, though they hadn't descended all that deep. The point had been to escape the explosion.

She followed Kirk up toward the light and then she was ahead of him. When she turned to see if he would follow, Kirk was fighting another diver. Shock ricocheted through her. Where had this man come from? Was it his job to make sure they died if the explosions hadn't been enough?

Even in the murky water she couldn't miss the glistening knife. A scream lodged in her throat. The diver went for Kirk's regulator hose. Kirk used his own diver's knife as the attacker sliced through the water with his weapon—his deadly intent clear. Bubbles roiled around them as they fought.

Cora frantically looked around the waters surrounding them. Abundant sea life swam nearby and ignored the battling divers as if they were simply part of the usual scenery. But Cora didn't care about the sea creatures—she searched for other attackers while a million questions jammed her thoughts all at once. Who had rigged the explosions on the *Sea Dragon*? Who was trying to kill them now? And why? She focused back on Kirk and his attacker.

Come on, Kirk! Lord, please help him!

She had never been trained to defend herself against such an attack. Had God sent Kirk for just this occasion? To protect Cora from those who would harm her?

What do they want from me?

Kirk swam backward in a defensive move. The other

diver was getting the upper hand. Her heart hammered and her rapid breaths would use up the oxygen in her tank too fast.

He needed her help, but she didn't know what to do. The two men's fighting skills—make that underwater fighting skills—far outmatched what few defensive moves she knew. Any attempt on her part could cause more harm than good. Still, Cora swam closer to study the diver. Did she know him?

His dry suit covered most of his face even behind the mask. The portion she might have seen remained shadowed. She couldn't get a good look at him, and his diving suit was typical black. There was nothing distinguishable about it. No designer emblem she could make out.

Suddenly her fears were realized. The attacker gained the advantage and sliced through Kirk's regulator hose. Bubbles rose violently.

The scene left Cora stunned. Kirk couldn't breathe. Her protector was going to die. They were *both* going to die.

Once again fear squeezed her lungs. Cora forced herself to breathe. If she were to help Kirk, she had to survive. In order to help him, she'd need to buddy breathe with him.

The attacker turned his mask, his face and attention on Cora. Thoughts of saving Kirk escaped like air bubbles rising to the surface.

The attacker hovered in the water with the knife as if catching his breath before slicing through the water toward her faster than she could have imagined.

Panic seized what was left of her already shallow breaths.

She'd die if she didn't breathe. Kirk would die if she didn't stay with him.

Survival instincts kicked in, overpowering her thoughts—rational or otherwise. Cora fled the scene.

She swam away, kicking her legs with everything in her. Years ago, she'd been a swimming champion. If nothing else, she could outswim him, even if this was technically scuba.

As she hurried away, leaving Kirk behind to fend for himself—a man who had saved her life twice now—guilt chased her. Part of her wanted to face the attacker to find out who he was. Why he wanted her dead. But the answer to that question didn't matter if she didn't survive. She focused on swimming, but it was her dream all over again.

Beneath the surface, the Salish Sea felt thick and gooey. Cora's limbs tired with her efforts. She could get nowhere.

God, help me! Help Kirk. Help us survive.

Cora didn't dare turn and look back, her only thought to escape. Would her life end in a horrible battle to breathe? Or with a quick flick of a diver's knife to her gut?

Memories flashed from the darkness, the shadows in her mind. An impression of what happened before, but fuzzy.

The present pushed the memories away as arms grabbed her from behind. She thrashed against her assailant. Whipping around as quickly as water allowed, she pulled her diver's knife out and thrust it at her would-be killer.

Kirk pulled the diver away from Cora before he could hurt her, and stabbed his knife into the other diver's leg. His eyes wide, he turned and swam off, blood spilling into the ocean. Kirk knew he should chase him down and restrain him. Detain him. Whatever it took to stop the madness. But his one breath wouldn't last much longer. He feared, too, that Cora was hurt. He hoped not fatally. She'd already escaped death twice today.

She had continued to swim away, not realizing that he'd fought the other diver off and needed her help. He could swim to the surface to breathe, but he would lose her if he didn't go after her. And if he didn't catch her? He would drown.

Furiously, he swam, his lungs burning. Just when he was certain he'd made a mistake in pursuing her, he caught up with her and grabbed her.

But she swung around again with her diver's knife, not realizing it was him this time. She barely missed him. Behind the mask her face filled with shock and relief.

His lungs burned. He gestured to her regulator, hoping his desperate message would be clear. He was about to run out of air.

She immediately offered the mouthpiece, and he eagerly took it and drew in the life-giving oxygen. Relief swelled with the air in his lungs. Once the panic eased away from his muscles, he looked her over. Good. She was okay. He glanced at their surroundings, though visibility wasn't great, to make sure the other diver was truly gone.

Kirk pointed to the surface. They would buddy breathe their way up and hopefully make it all the way this time. And then what? As they shared what was left of her oxygen, the water around them turned crimson.

Blood.

And blood would draw sharks.

The wound where the attacker had gouged Kirk's

arm burned like fire from the cold salt water. Without oxygen, his only thought had been to breathe, oh, yeah, and save Cora. He'd forgotten he'd been slashed.

He pressed his palm over the gash. He would survive the wound—that was, if the blood didn't draw unwanted creatures of the deep, or the cold didn't get to him. With his suit compromised, it was as if he wasn't wearing it at all. He sliced off a piece of his suit and fashioned a tourniquet. That should stanch the blood for at least a little while. His diver's watch indicated they were good to continue slowly upward. He'd had no choice but to rush them away from the blast as far as possible.

As they ascended, Kirk remained guarded, watching for another diver who might try to kill them.

He suspected that someone had remained behind to kill them if they survived the explosions—the diver he'd just fought off. But he didn't know if another diver would come for them. He studied Cora as she shared her limited oxygen with him, her bright eyes determined. Did she have any idea how much danger she was in? By the fear surging in her gaze, he thought she just might.

Regrettably, he doubted she knew why. That was something Kirk had to find out. Fierce protectiveness rose up inside—he had to keep Cora safe. Protect her at all costs. He could only hope to do that if he found out who was responsible and why, and maybe that would lead him to answers about what had happened to Drake, as well.

Finally, they breached the surface. He drew in a long breath, savoring the smell of the salty ocean—and life. The sun shone brightly, breaking through the clouds on a summer day, belying the last few minutes of terror as though none of it had happened.

Flames licked the ocean where the sheen of oil and remnants of the hull that had yet to sink remained. Cora bobbed in the choppy water next to him. Kirk held her close so they wouldn't get separated.

His only goal over the last few minutes had been to survive.

Survive the bomb.

Survive the attacker.

Survive the deep.

But now?

Her mask pulled to rest on top of her head, Cora let her regulator dangle. Lines were carved into her pretty forehead and between her brows. Kirk gripped both arms to look her in the eyes, though the swells and surges of the open waters of the Salish Sea made that hard. In a million years, he never would have imagined this moment. Him floating in the water—in the middle of nowhere for all practical purposes—with Cora Strand, who was counting on him to save her, to protect her. She might not put that into words, but he saw it in her eyes all the same. And for some weird reason, his mouth twisted up in a half grin.

Who would have thought? Who could have known?

God. God knew...

But Cora gave him an accusing glare, and he read her easily enough—*how can you grin at a time like this?* He quickly dropped the grin, trading it for an expression more reflective of their current state.

"Are you okay?" What a question for him to ask. How could she truly answer that? Still, he'd clarify. "I'm asking if you're physically hurt."

Water lapped over her face and into her mouth. She choked it up. "I don't think so."

In her eyes, he saw that she had a thousand questions about what had just transpired. He had questions of his own. Had she remembered what happened earlier in the day when he'd dragged her from the ocean, lost to this world? It seemed like forever ago. But someone had tried to kill her and Kirk was hard-pressed to understand who and why. What had started out as a search for answers regarding Drake Jackson had turned into something even more deadly and sinister.

Her gaze flashed with fear. He sensed a part of her was afraid of him as well, and remembered she'd asked him if he'd killed Trip. He wished he hadn't remembered that just now. His insides roiled with the accusation.

How could she even consider that a possibility? If he were honest, on some personal level, it hurt, jabbed at his heart more than it should. After all, their relationship had ended long ago, thanks to his brother.

Upon thinking about how his brother had treated her, his frown deepened. She might actually hold Kirk responsible, since he'd introduced her to Stephan to begin with. Kirk wanted her to know that he wasn't his brother Stephan, but that seemed completely out of context at the moment, especially since they still weren't out of danger.

"What now, Kirk?" Cora's question brought his thoughts back to their current predicament. "How do we get to safety? We don't have enough oxygen to get to the island beneath the surface, even if that man hadn't cut your hose. I'm a great swimmer, or at least, I used to be. But even so, I can't swim all the way to Farrow Island."

Cora continued asking questions, stating the obvious and detailing their predicament. She hadn't stopped talking long enough for him to give her answers. Just as well. He was still formulating a plan. He'd set one in motion days ago when he'd gotten that niggling feeling that things were about to go south and fast.

Kirk watched the sea and the horizon.

Waited. Maybe he should grab some of the debris that had remained floating so they would have something to hold on to in addition to the buoyancy vests that kept them floating with all their scuba gear.

She popped him on the arm. "Are you even listening?"

He nodded. "I heard everything you said."

She pursed her lips. Blinked seawater from her eyes. She was afraid and vulnerable. Maybe it was wrong of him, but he didn't think she'd ever been more beautiful. Inside, he berated himself—he shouldn't have those kinds of thoughts about her, especially at the worst time possible.

They still had a long way to go before their survival was assured.

"What are you thinking?" she asked. "I want to know how we're getting out of this."

"Look, I'm making this up as I go. I didn't expect to find a bomb." A little honesty never hurt, though maybe he shouldn't have been so brutally frank.

"What about the attacker down there? Did you expect him?"

"Why would I expect him? I don't know what is going on, either."

Kirk peered downward, but couldn't see past the surface. What was going on in the murky waters beneath them that was worth so much? That had cost a research vessel? Drake. Trip. Lance. Who else would have to die before this was over—whatever *this* was?

Cora...

He looked at her beautiful features, those eyes that had caught his attention the first day he saw her. Warmth flooded his gut. The sudden urge to pull her against him as they floated, to hold and shelter her, came over him. He reached for her and held her loosely now, but he wanted to gather her close. He shoved the errant thought away. But he wouldn't let go of the fierce protectiveness that had been ignited.

It just might keep them alive.

Seagulls wailed and cawed in the blue sky above, reminding him land was close and yet too far.

A wave engulfed them, catching him off guard, and ripped Cora from him. She coughed up water as he swam for her. A chunk of the vessel drifted by and he caught it. Cora joined him to hold on to what looked like it could have been a cabinet from the galley. Their vests did the work of keeping them afloat, but holding on to something brought a measure of added security.

"Okay, so you don't know what's going on any more than I do," she said. "Believe it or not, I'm not blaming you, Kirk."

"Aren't you? You accused me of killing Trip."

"I don't know what to think about any of this, but despite my accusation, despite holding that knife, deep down, I could never believe you would do such a thing. I was just...scared, okay? If I had really thought you murdered Trip, I wouldn't have asked if you did. Saying that would put me in too-stupid-to-live territory. Maybe I'm wrong, but I don't see myself as that stupid, so, yeah, I wouldn't have confronted you."

There she went, babbling again. Talking too much. Nerves. She was nervous. Still, it was kind of endearing. And he saw well enough in her eyes that she couldn't think anyone she *knew* could do it, not just that Kirk was innocent of that crime. But clearly someone had. Even though she denied it, Cora held on to doubts about him, as well. But he had a feeling it went far beyond the situation involving murder.

"I'm glad you trust me, Cora, but for now it's probably best if you aren't so trusting of anyone."

Her eyes widened.

"Don't get me wrong. I *want* you to trust me—we're going to need to trust each other through this—but we need to keep our guards up. Obviously, someone we know is behind this."

"Unless...unless someone else climbed aboard the *Sea Dragon* and killed Trip and set the bombs."

Admittedly, that scenario hadn't even occurred to him. He'd only been able to think about the men who'd been diving with Cora when she went missing, or at least they had claimed she'd gone missing. Someone had tried to kill her. Those men had left Kirk and Cora and two others on the vessel to be obliterated—Trip and Lance. Granted, Trip was already dead. He didn't buy the theory that someone they didn't know had come aboard and planted bombs. He already had enough guilty parties in mind.

"Right, but I saw the captain rowing away mere minutes before the bombs were due to go off." There was the matter of Coburn and Trip...but Trip had been murdered, according to Cora. Had Coburn killed his partner in crime before heading to the island where he'd be safe and sound while the *Sea Dragon* was blown sky high?

"I don't… I can't believe he's behind this. I've known him too long. There's no way. That was just a coincidence. Besides, it doesn't matter right now," she said. "We need to find a way out of this water. It's cold, even in the summer. We can only last so long, even though we're in dry suits, and the blood…"

Sharks.

"Someone was bound to have seen the explosion." He hoped that someone was his friend Judd. Earlier Kirk had set a plan in motion and was glad he had listened to his gut about the growing tension on the *Sea Dragon*, and the need for an escape plan. His buddy would arrive soon if he'd seen the explosion.

"While that might be true, we can't be sure. I don't feel confident we can make it to the island, but we have our vests to help us float and that could help. I think we should at least try to swim to Farrow. It's better than waiting here."

"I disagree. We'll wait here, near the explosion. Someone will come." He was counting on it.

"Who put you in charge, Kirk? I'd prefer to start swimming because we need to let the crew know what's happened as soon as possible. Let the authorities know about the murder and attempted murders."

"And what if someone from the crew is responsible?" Like Coburn. Captain Menken.

"We can let the authorities figure that out."

A wave washed over them. Cora's lips were turning blue. He was chilled to the bone, too, but he forced her to look at him. "Listen to me. Right now, except for the diver who attacked us, whoever tried to kill us thinks we're dead."

Realization slowly dawned in Cora's beautiful green-flecked hazel eyes. "They think we're dead? Others will think that, too. We have to let someone know we're alive! My family will be devastated when they hear the news the *Sea Dragon* was destroyed."

"Not so fast, Cora." He had to persuade her.

Cora opened her mouth, presumably to argue with him, but a boat approached. The boat he hoped for? Yes, yes it was. Relief flooded through him. They would make it.

The *Clara Steele* headed their way, captained by Judd Verone, an old friend from Kirk's time in the navy. He waved with both arms.

"Is this someone we can trust, Kirk?"

"Yes. He's an old friend."

He'd run into Judd after he'd taken this job on the *Sea Dragon*. His friend lived on the Lopez Islands and fished in the area. Without a doubt, Kirk knew he could trust the man. After what they'd been through together, Judd was closer than any brother. That was especially true in Kirk's case.

When Kirk had sensed the tension running high and time running out, he had asked Judd to stay close, if possible, in case he needed a quick escape. From Judd's boat, they could call the Coast Guard and inform them of the explosion. Kirk could communicate freely with his NCIS superior, Matt, as well as with Drake's father, Commander Jackson, who'd requested Kirk be given this assignment. They could head for Farrow Island as well, to inform the crew—at least, the innocent crew members if there were any—and that was a problem. He wasn't sure who to tell. At this point, everyone was a suspect.

Kirk was still weighing their options. His priority

had shifted from finding out what happened to Drake to protecting Cora. She had to know something worth killing for. He suspected that whatever she knew was also tied to Drake's disappearance. At least, that was his working theory at this juncture.

Choppy waves worked against them, carrying them away from the approaching trawler even as the *Clara Steele* chugged through the waters toward them.

"I'm glad he's a friend," she said. "But I almost wouldn't care if he was another bad guy. I'm ready to be dry and warm."

Kirk chuckled at her small joke. "We're going to be okay, Cora. But…do you remember anything yet from earlier today?"

She slowly shook her head. "Only an impression. I… You don't think it was an accident, do you?"

It was his turn to shake his head. If she knew that her hose had been cut, she wouldn't even have to ask. "I wish I did. But I think that someone wants you dead." And she'd nearly drowned. He suspected the cold water temperatures had played a part in her survival. While performing CPR he'd prayed every second that he wasn't too late.

He knew the moment that the truth registered in her eyes—the shock of it. "I admit I was hoping you wouldn't say that. That…that was the impression I have. Someone wants me dead." Tears pooled in her eyes, making her appear all the more waterlogged.

"But why, Cora? Why would someone go to this much trouble to kill you?"

THREE

Someone wants me dead.

The words pounded through her head. She studied the man in a diver's suit and scuba gear, floating on the frigid waves with her as they waited for the trawler. The boat was taking entirely too long to get to them.

Cora had already reasoned that if Kirk had wanted her dead, then he'd surely had his chance, and instead, he'd saved her twice. Even so, that didn't mean he wasn't responsible for what was going on now—the bombs on the *Sea Dragon* or for Trip's murder, even if indirectly. In fact, she got the feeling that he was somehow involved even as another part of her said he couldn't be.

Cora held her breath as a swell washed over her. She eyed Kirk—his surfer good looks, his strong, muscular physique and intelligent blue eyes.

Maybe it was more that she didn't *want* to believe he was involved. But who could be behind any of this? She knew the scientists and crew of the *Sea Dragon*. Had worked with them for six months. Was just settling into her job and had a good feeling about her future—that she'd finally made it.

Her life and all she had worked for were finally coming together.

Then Kirk had entered her world, dredging up old feelings she wanted to forget. And now…

Now this.

Her heart jumped around inside, the irregular beat making her uneasy.

Kirk continued to look at her, expecting an answer about who would go to all this trouble to kill her.

"You ask a good question. I have no idea." As the waves rocked her, Cora let the shock of all that had happened over the last hour roll through her.

The boat continued to approach them as islands of fire still burned, oil-soaked fragments of the research vessel that could very well burn through the night.

But eventually the orange and yellow flames that seemed to float on the water would die out and any evidence that the *Sea Dragon* had been here would sink to the ocean floor. The remnants of the research vessel would lie there until divers explored it—not for the remains of a shipwreck of antiquity to be put on the record books for the state of Washington, but for evidence of crimes committed.

Murder and more.

Kirk watched her—concern and compassion pouring from his piercing blue gaze. And something more—knowledge. It was just like she'd suspected. He knew something about all of this. The thought sent apprehension spiking through her again.

He frowned as though reading her thoughts, sensing her doubts, and though he appeared unwilling to pull his gaze from her, the fishing trawler drew his attention away. Slowly, Kirk lifted his face upward.

"Looks like you need a ride," a man called from the boat.

"Judd!" Kirk shouted to the beefy man who leaned over the railing from the deck. "You couldn't have come at a better time."

"So how is it that your friend just happened to show up here?" Cora asked.

"He fishes these parts." Kirk took hold of the ladder then glanced at her. "I ran into him a few weeks back. We're old navy buddies."

Pure relief swelled inside. Finally, they were catching a break. "Come to think of it, I might have seen him around, too. Maybe on Farrow Island."

Kirk gestured for Cora to go up the ladder first. She was clumsy and awkward in the heavy scuba gear as she climbed up the ladder. Kirk was right behind, watching her ungraceful ways, and *of course* she had to slip on the top rung!

"I got you." Kirk caught her by the vest and steadied her, pushing her onward.

The fisherman who could moonlight as a lumberjack—Judd, was it?—assisted her the rest of the way up, practically lifting her off her feet and setting her on his deck.

So she'd had a misstep, she could handle herself. Still, it was good to know someone had your back. "Thanks, guys."

Cora began the laborious process of disentangling herself from the scuba gear.

Kirk hopped on the deck and shrugged out of his tank.

A gusty breeze whipped across the deck as the boat rocked. Even in her dry suit, she shivered. Anxiety

caused a chill that entwined with the frigid temperatures of the sea from which she'd emerged, still drip-
ping seawater. It might be summer in this part of the
world, but the water temps could fool people—to their
detriment. Cold water shock could kill. And she'd been
floating in it longer than she would have liked, especially if she added in the effects of being thrown from
the *Sea Dragon* by the concussive force of a bomb.

"It's okay, Cora. It's going to be okay." Kirk gripped
her arms, stared down at her as he leaned in, his tone
gentle and reassuring. He was so close his warm breath
fanned her cheeks.

Wanting to believe him, she nodded.

But, truth be told, she was unconvinced. She shrugged
out of his loose hold and moved away, doubting he believed his own words. How could it be okay? Trip had
been murdered. Lance was dead, too. They would have
seen him floating out there, the same as them, if he had
survived that blast.

Someone had tried to kill them.

Kirk closed the distance again. "We made it, Cora.
We survived the blast and the attack diver. It's a start.
We can regroup and go from there."

We? She wasn't sure she should be going anywhere
with Kirk once she reached the island. Sure protectiveness poured from him. He'd done just that—protected
her when he'd rescued her from the ocean depths and
revived her, then saved them from the explosion that had
destroyed the *Sea Dragon*. And until Cora resolved who
wanted her dead and why, sticking close to Kirk Higgins
might just be the safest place for her. But it definitely
wasn't the safest place for her heart. Unfortunately, she
was still attracted to him, even after all this time. She

was vulnerable to him. She reminded herself that he let her down, hurt her deeply before. He could let her down again, at least in matters of the heart.

She covered her eyes for a moment, taking everything in. Comprehending the tragic chain of events that had brought them to this point would take some time. When she opened her eyes again, Judd was pulling the ladder up.

Kirk studied her, that same worried look on his handsome face. Admittedly, it wasn't a look she'd ever seen from Stephan—who, now that she thought about it, was all about himself. She wasn't a great judge of character or how else could she have let herself get involved with him?

"What happened out there?" Judd asked.

"I'll tell you everything as soon as we get dry," Kirk said.

"Good idea. Let's get you guys belowdecks and into some warm clothes. Then, when you're nice and toasty, you can tell me all about it. Looks like you need some first aid there, too, buddy."

The blood still seeped from Kirk's wound.

Kirk nodded. "We need to call the Coast Guard. Likely the automatic emergency beacons were destroyed with the explosion before a distress signal was sent."

"Already done," Judd said.

"Good, that's good." Kirk's expression didn't match his words. "But...I don't think we can wait around here for them."

Judd angled his head, suspicion in his dark eyes.

"Someone tried to kill us," Cora said. "I don't want to stay here for someone to try again. You could be in danger, too, for helping us. They boarded the *Sea Dragon* and planted a bomb."

Cora ignored the funny look that Kirk gave her, but she had a hard time believing it was anyone from the group of people she'd worked with for the last six months.

"Well, I can't argue with that plan," Judd said. "I'll take us out and away. Kirk, you need me to dress that wound?"

"Maybe. I'll see what I can do when I change, and if I can't handle it, then you or Cora can help."

Judd gestured below. "The first-aid kit is in the head. After you guys change into something warm, meet me in the galley for something hot to drink. A cup of joe or some hot chocolate should take the chill off." He eyed her up and down. "Sorry, miss, but you won't find anything small enough."

"I'm sure I can make anything I find work. And thank you for rescuing us."

After removing the rest of the scuba gear, Cora followed Kirk belowdecks. He started for a closet, but she redirected him to the head.

"Let's get the first-aid kit and look at your arm first. Personally, I can't stand the sight of blood." An image of Trip's blood flashed in her mind.

Hold it together.

Nodding, Kirk cut off the neoprene tourniquet he'd crafted from the sleeve of his dry suit to expose the gash in his arm. She cleaned it off and tried to ignore how near she was to him. Heat emanated from his body and she couldn't help but want to get closer to that warmth, but tried to keep her distance. His muscular biceps and broad shoulders worked to disarm her and draw her in.

"That's probably going to need some stitches, but this will have to do for now." She applied antibiotic ointment and closed the slash with a butterfly bandage, then wrapped it with Coban self-adherent wrap.

"You do good work." The way he smiled and the way his eyes roamed her face sent her backing against the wall.

Kirk led her out of the head and found the master stateroom. He opened the closet doors and looked inside. Cora waited. Looking through someone else's things was awkward, so she'd leave Kirk to it.

He tossed her sweats and a hoodie, then continued searching. She held up the oversize clothing made for a ginormous man.

"What do you think he is? Six feet five inches? Two hundred fifty pounds of pure muscle?" she asked.

Kirk arched a brow.

With his lean, muscular physique, Kirk was every bit as masculine and had the perfect body for a diver. He knew that, and she had no doubt that he was aware she knew it.

"No, really. That guy is scary big. I have no idea how I can make these clothes work."

A half smile hitched up Kirk's strong, scruffy jaw. "It's just for a little while. We'll get you something new to wear."

"Where? Farrow Island?"

The thought brought her back to their real predicament. Emotion thickened her voice. "We need to tell the others. I know we don't know who to trust, but their lives could be in danger, too. We also need to talk to the authorities."

Kirk dropped the jeans and shirt he'd found on the

twin bed and pressed his hands on her shoulders, which was quickly becoming a familiar gesture from him. "And we will. But first things first. The three basics for survival. Shelter, water and food." He dropped his hands from her shoulders to grab her hands and rub them. "Your hands are like ice. Let's get something warm in us. We'll regroup and strategize."

His nearness, his intense gaze, did strange things to her insides. Well, not strange, exactly, but familiar stirrings. Unwelcome and unbidden. She absolutely couldn't get distracted by this handsome, broad-shouldered diver extraordinaire. Of all the crew members, she knew Kirk the least, even though she'd known him the longest. She had never forgotten the day that she'd bumped into him in the hallway at U of W. He'd been a senior. She was in her second semester. They'd been taking the same speech class. All the books she was carrying, because her backpack had broken, had scattered on the floor when they'd collided.

Kirk had blamed himself, apologized and helped her pick them up, then asked her to dinner. She'd already noticed him across the room. Shared a look and a smile and the rest was history. They started slow at first— hanging out at football games. Then the beach. She loved walking the beach with him. They shared a deep connection, or at least she had thought.

Then came the day when Kirk introduced her to his brother, Stephan. The guy was all charm and charisma and knew how to move in, even talking about taking her to dinner as if to seal the deal. Cora had sort of waited around for Kirk to let Stephan know she was dating him, but the next thing she knew, he had left her there with Stephan. She was confused and hurt. In high school, she'd been dumped at the prom, and over a decade later that memory still stung. To her, Kirk had practically done the same thing by leaving her with his brother as soon as the guy showed an interest in her. She'd been flattered—two brothers interested—except Kirk hadn't really been interested because, if he had been, he wouldn't have left her with Stephan. He would have stood up for her. Was it so wrong that she'd expected more from him? She had thought they had something going—and maybe even the hint of the promise of a future.

Somehow, nine months later, she'd ended up almost engaged to his lying brother.

Bottom line, she wouldn't trust her insane attraction to Kirk with any remote part of her heart, even the deepest part that believed it had always been Kirk. But with her life—how far could she trust him, given the current state of events that had thrown them together again?

"Say it, Cora. Just say what you're thinking."

She wanted to shrink back from him. How could he read her so easily?

"You're still afraid of me." Hurt skirted the edge of his dark blue gaze.

Why would he be hurt? Frowning, he looked up to the ceiling of the stateroom then at her again.

She would have stepped back but the wall prevented her. "You're the one who told me not to trust anyone."

"You're right. I did."

His answer disappointed her. Scared her.

He released her hands. No longer reassuring her? He scraped his fingers down his jaw. "I'm not going to hurt you. You can count on me to protect you."

"But I can't trust you?"

"I only want you to remain cautious. Don't get in the habit of trusting. That's all I meant. You made friends on the *Sea Dragon*. Any one of them could be a murderer. You were diving with Coburn and Trip when you ended up nearly losing your life. See what I'm saying?"

She nodded. But she couldn't see either of them trying to harm her, and Trip had been murdered...

"But you have questions. Go ahead and ask."

Cora swallowed hard. She shouldn't. She really shouldn't, but the question burned through her. She would have at least this answer. "I saw you leave Trip's room just before I found him dead in the computer room. What were you doing?"

Well, at least now he understood her uncertainty about his innocence. That would definitely look extremely suspicious. He'd had a good reason to be in Trip's room but how did he tell her?

She studied him. Could she read him as well as he could read her?

Oh, man. Hold it together now. Do not let her see that you're hiding something.

Though he didn't *want* to hide it—he wanted to tell her everything—Kirk knew he couldn't blow his cover, even with Cora. Even though her life was in danger.

And spilling the truth to her now would undoubtedly worsen the tension that had been festering between them ever since he'd come aboard the *Sea Dragon*. He recalled that she'd been as shocked to see him as he'd been when he'd found out she was the archaeologist on board. He didn't blame her for not wanting to have anything to do with him. She probably resented his appearance in her perfect world—connected to the dream job she'd wanted. He remembered at least that much from their short time together. And, in all honesty, she had every right to harbor those feelings—especially after everything Stephan had put her through. He was ashamed of his brother and wished he could tell her the whole of that now.

But it was water under the bridge, as the saying went, and there was no point in dredging it up now. He couldn't know if her guarded reaction to him was because of their past or because of their current predicament. Maybe a little of both. Still, she somehow managed to also be completely transparent—something he was definitely not being with her. At some point, when she learned the truth, she would think him a liar.

Like Stephan.

I'm nothing like my brother.

He and Stephan were polar opposites—but the guy had stolen her from him. And Kirk, to his great regret, had let him do it.

"Well?" she repeated, jarring him out of his thoughts. "What were you doing in his room?"

It took some effort, but Kirk didn't allow himself to flinch at her question since she was clearly gauging his reaction. But, obviously, the fact that she'd spied him leaving Trip's quarters definitely wasn't what he wanted to hear from her.

But since he couldn't tell her that he was an undercover NCIS agent, he obviously had to tread carefully here. His goal was to find out what he could about Drake Jackson's disappearance. He owed it to his best friend to find out. If he'd learned anything in his experience, it was that one never knew who they could completely trust. He could have it all wrong—Cora could somehow be involved in whatever was going on and hiding that fact. She could very well know who wanted her dead and why. But especially if she was innocent in all of this—the less she knew, the safer she would be.

Still, at the moment, he had to come up with an explanation and he'd been stalling too long.

"Kirk?" She cocked a brow. "Are you going to answer me or not?" If she really thought he was the murderer, she sure didn't act that afraid of him. Just a little wary.

"Yes, I will. But first, take me back to the scene of the crime, beginning with when you found him dead."

"Murdered." Her eyes glistened again. "He had a knife in his chest...blood was everywhere." She blinked away tears, holding it together. "Trip and I were close. We were friends." She glared at him, as though wanting to accuse him again, but he knew it was more that she wanted to accuse someone—anyone—and her anger at the senseless murder had found a target, that was all.

He drew in a slow breath. His heart went out to her. He hated that she'd found Trip like that. Without thinking, he reached up and stroked her soft cheek with the backs of his fingers. She closed her eyes as if soaking in his reassurance. The lines in her face softened as her anger melted away. He thought she might let the tears go. If so, then Kirk would have no choice but to pull her into his arms. He wanted to hold her as it was, but he would deny himself that pleasure as long as possible. After all, Cora had made her choice long ago.

And she'd chosen Stephan.

Her eyes slid open and she took a step back. He dropped his hand, already missing the feel of her skin.

"I told you what I saw. Now answer me. Why were you in his room?"

The suspicion in her gaze twisted his insides. "I was looking for a tool. Trip had it in his hands yesterday, and I couldn't find it. I know it was wrong for me to go into his room without permission. But I didn't figure he would mind since I needed it." He was glad for the reasonable explanation, which he had concocted as his excuse on the remote chance he got caught. But he hadn't really imagined someone would see him, since most everyone had gone ashore and Cora was supposed to have been resting in her room after her close call with death.

A shudder ran over her.

"You should get changed. Get some color back into your cheeks." He needed to put an end to the conversation before she dragged something out of him he wasn't prepared to give. Besides, she *did* need to get dressed and warm.

Kirk left her in the stateroom and found another. He changed out of the dry suit and into the jeans and a shirt.

He needed to contact Matt and let him know about the discovery and what had happened, but something gnawed at the back of his mind. He had the gut feeling his cover had been blown and that's why the research vessel had been destroyed, leaving behind no evidence. If the blast had gone as planned, Cora and Kirk would have been perceived as accidental casualties with no one to question otherwise. The same for Lance and Trip.

In Trip's room, Kirk had hacked into his computer and found a suspicious communication. A code name and a location. A code name and location for what? A dead drop? But if someone knew he was undercover, and had blown up the *Sea Dragon* to cover their tracks, how had they found out? He wasn't one hundred percent sure that contacting Matt with the information he'd unearthed was the right way to go at this juncture. Though he didn't like where his thoughts were leading him, he couldn't deny the possibility someone Kirk knew was involved in what was going down here.

Matt hadn't wanted him involved in this assignment, but Jackson had connections and had pulled some strings. So, Kirk reasoned, he should contact Commander Jackson first because he had no doubt about trusting Drake's father—and a man he had looked up to more than his own dad, who considered Kirk a complete disappointment.

Commander Jackson had not only pulled strings to get Kirk in position on the *Sea Dragon*, where Drake had last worked, but in a sense, Commander Jackson was also in charge of Kirk's undercover operation. Though, technically, Kirk was a civilian, as were his supervisor and NCIS colleagues.

However, first things first—he needed to get his hands on a communication device.

Hopefully the Coast Guard had found the burning remnants of the *Sea Dragon* by now.

Exiting the stateroom, Kirk knocked on the door behind which he'd left Cora. It was cracked open enough that he could see inside and he noticed the room was empty. Voices resounded down the hallway. Kirk found her talking to Judd in the galley. Kirk hung back and watched. Judd winked at Cora and she actually blushed as she accepted a mug of hot chocolate. While he was glad to see the rush of color into her pale cheeks…

Jealousy slithered across Kirk's heart.

A completely inappropriate reaction. Before he revealed himself, he tamped down the surge of emotion. Judd wasn't Stephan. Nor could he steal Cora from Kirk—she and Kirk weren't in a relationship. She couldn't be taken from him.

But she could be killed if he didn't hold her close.

FOUR

As she sat in the galley, listening to Judd, exhaustion pressed in on Cora's mind and body, but she had no idea what to do next. So she waited for someone else to come up with a plan of action. But how could she trust it was the right thing? Sure, they could go to Farrow Island and tell the authorities, but she had a feeling it would be more than a meager handful of law enforcement officers could handle. She and Kirk could be dead before she finished telling her story.

Come on, Cora, think...

Maybe something would come to her as she sat in the galley with Judd and waited for Kirk—why had he taken longer to get dressed than she had?

The *Clara Steele* wasn't the typical workhorse fishing trawler that smelled of the ocean and dead fish and sweaty men and dirty socks. The walls weren't grimy or an ugly green in need of a new coat of paint. Instead, it looked like Judd had been working on the boat to fix it up and make it nice. Considering the comfortable seating and modern kitchen in the galley, maybe he lived on the boat.

He'd anchored the *Clara Steele* a good distance from

where the *Sea Dragon* had gone down, for which she was grateful. But dread and fear remained at the edge of her mind. At this moment, even Judd's bulk could intimidate Cora. And she would have been if it weren't for his charming smile and a sense of humor that could have made her laugh on any other day, but not in the midst of the traumatic events of the last few hours.

Still, Cora attempted to relax as the big man told her a handful of lame jokes while he typed on his computer. Checking email? Mapping out coordinates? She didn't know. But he kept trying to cheer her up. She couldn't blame him for that, so in return, she tried to smile, but she couldn't bring herself to laugh.

His dark eyes studied her. "It's not working, huh?"

She sagged. "I'm sorry." He hadn't been through what she'd been through. He hadn't seen a crewmate lying in his own blood, a knife wound to his chest. Or had the research vessel where he'd worked blown to bits.

Thoughts of the grim situation could drag her down and drown her if she let them. How did she rise above this? Keep going when grief held her prisoner?

In a way, all that had happened was similar to her dream—or rather, nightmare.

She shuddered as the dream tried to wrap around her, but cacophonous sounds drew her back to the moment. Through a porthole, she heard seagulls squabbling over the latest catch, their caws one of many usual sounds she'd expect to hear on a normal day. Except there was *nothing* normal about this day.

Add to that, she and Kirk could still be in danger. She sipped and smiled at Judd, but only listened with half an ear. She hoped they would be safe here for the moment.

"How about some more hot chocolate?" He reached for her mug.

"Okay, sure."

She watched him pull the box out of the cabinet stocked with canned food—chicken, beef stew, chili and coffee. A minute passed before he handed her the mug refueled with the mixture of hot water and a packet of hot chocolate mix. "Thanks."

He frowned. This was getting kind of awkward. She sank deeper into the booth and sipped.

"What's taking Kirk so long? Did he decide to take a nap?" Judd's deep robust laugh demanded her full attention.

Something about the man's sense of humor seemed strange to her coming from such a big guy with a deep voice. Or maybe she was too tired to make sense of it.

The warm galley of the fishing boat, along with the hot chocolate, were quickly having an effect on her. Her lids grew heavy. Her will to remain alert and survive was losing to exhaustion. Over the rim of the warm mug, she spotted Kirk hanging back in the hallway, watching her. What was that about?

She sipped, then lowered the cup. "Well, what are you waiting for?"

Judd swung around to smile at his buddy and offer him a warm mug, as well. Kirk approached, took it and drank, his blue eyes dark and disturbing. Cora focused back on Judd.

She was more than grateful that Judd had shown up when he had, though it seemed a little convenient. She hated that she constantly jumped to negative conclusions, but after the last few hours, she couldn't help herself. And it was just good plain common sense for her to remain guarded.

Hard to do when it came to Kirk, who slid into the booth next to her, close enough she could feel the heat radiate from his fit, muscled body. She really wanted to lean into him.

She set the mug down and frowned.

"You're welcome to lie down in one of the state-rooms. Get some rest. You both look exhausted." Judd refilled Kirk's cup, with black coffee this time. *They must know each other pretty well.*

Cora was about to protest Judd's suggestion when a yawn took hold.

Kirk gently touched her arm. "Why don't you go ahead?"

"No, I'm okay," she lied. *I'm afraid to sleep. Afraid to dream.* A shiver crawled over her.

"I'm here, Cora. I'll protect you. Do you trust me?" Kirk's blue gaze—now soft and tender—searched hers.

She shouldn't trust anyone. That's what he'd said, but he hadn't meant himself, and she understood that. *I want to...* "It's not that I don't trust you."

He took her hand and squeezed. She could feel the strength in his grip and it gave her a measure of comfort, except his next words took it away. "Look, this might not be over yet. You need to get your rest while you can. I need to make some calls and see what's going on. Judd is here with me to make sure nobody tries to come aboard and cause more harm. So please, Cora, rest those pretty eyes."

Pretty eyes? She wasn't sure how to take that comment. She was perfectly capable of waiting up with him, but on the other hand, he was right. She wouldn't be at her best if she didn't rest. She stared into his eyes searching for something she could grab hold of—truth, yes, there it was in his eyes. Truth and trust—she would trust him to keep her safe while she did as he asked. She was losing the battle as it was.

"Well, only for a few moments. Come and get me up if you find out anything." To Judd, she said, "Are you taking us to Farrow Island now?"

"Sure. If Kirk agrees, then we'll be heading that way soon. And in that case, we'll probably be there when you wake up."

Cora finished her drink and stood from the booth, brushing by Kirk. Her legs trembled, her shakiness a consequence of the ordeal. She headed down the short passageway and went into the stateroom where she'd changed earlier.

"Cora," Kirk said from behind.

She hadn't realized he'd come after her. She turned around to find him, arms crossed, studying her once again.

"What are you doing? Why did you follow me?"

"Checking on you. You're swaying." He took a step closer.

The next thing she knew, she was in his embrace. She would have pushed away, but his muscled arms filled a deep abyss in her. His heart beat strong and steady. An irresistible combination for her desperate need. He hadn't been shaken like she had. Why was that, anyway? And wasn't he exhausted?

Wasn't he…scared?

"It's all right, Cora. It's going to be all right."

I'm not going to cry. I'm not going to cry.

Against his chest, strong and sure, she spoke. "People are dead, Kirk. Friends are dead. It's not all right. It's not going to be all right ever again."

He slowly eased away, but not enough to let her go. Just enough to look into her eyes. He was doing an awful lot of that lately. It was strange after they'd ignored each other as much as humanly possible for the last two months.

"I'm talking about *you*, Cora. Sure, this is devastating, but I'm going to make sure you're safe. That nobody is going to hurt you."

"Why are you so determined to protect me?" Why not pawn her off on the next person, which he could very well do? She wished she had the skills to protect herself, that way he wouldn't have to worry. Or was she assuming she was more important to him than she was? He would probably be protecting anyone at this point, not just her.

Feeling the heat in her cheeks again, she bit her lip and stepped fully away.

"You might prefer someone else to watch over you, Cora, but we're here together now. I'll keep you safe until the danger has passed." He nodded and left her standing there.

She couldn't exactly tell him she could keep herself safe. It wouldn't be true. She hadn't done that at least twice today. And she was such a jerk. In spite of her effort to keep things impersonal, she'd done just the opposite. She pushed the stateroom door shut, yanked back the blanket on the small twin bed and crawled beneath the covers. She was bone tired. She'd lost her battle with exhaustion, but what did it matter?

Like she could get any sleep.

* * *

Kirk didn't know what he was doing here. Being near Cora messed with his mind. He couldn't think clearly. He waited around the corner in the short, freshly painted passageway. When he heard the door shut, he released a slow, measured breath.

I'll keep you safe until the danger has passed. He hadn't exactly promised her, but he might as well have. And with that proclamation, he'd officially switched his priority from his mission to Cora—but that wasn't anything someone else in his position would do differently.

He hoped he was up to the task. He wasn't sure it was right to make her believe in him and that he could keep her safe when he wasn't entirely positive he could. And another thing, he shouldn't let her get to him the way he had.

Giving himself a moment, he squeezed his eyes shut and drew in a steadying breath. He shouldn't have held her like that.

Felt her warm, soft form against him. But how could he not reach out to her and offer comfort? She'd been visibly shaken. Crumbling right before his eyes. And it took a lot to shake Cora Strand—but today's events, almost dying twice, seeing Trip's murdered body, the *Sea Dragon* destroyed—would rock even the strongest person.

Anyone would have comforted her. Except Kirk wasn't anyone. Seeing her like that, well, he had acted on pure impulse. Adding to the growing pile of his troubles, he wasn't sure how to keep himself emotionally disconnected from her, even when failing to do so would be a huge mistake.

But one thing he did know—he could pray.

Lord, please let her get some rest. Show me what to do. How to keep her safe. And maybe a little help finding out what is going on would be nice.

He had too many questions and no real answers, and a woman he had once imagined himself falling in love with to protect.

He'd never found himself in this kind of situation before or had to rely on his training in this way. He had a feeling the next few hours would push him to the edge of his skills.

He'd better be ready.

Even though he probably needed to rest and decompress, too, there wasn't time for that. His military training had taught him to run on fumes. Lives could depend on it. He went in search of Judd and found him on the deck outside the helm, peering through a pair of high-powered binoculars. Summer storm clouds brewed off to the west.

"See anything?" Kirk asked.

"Not yet." His buddy blew out a breath. Apparently he had more to say. "You asked me to hang around in the area for a few days. That was asking a lot, especially since you wouldn't tell me why. I almost went the other direction, man. If there hadn't been something in your voice that told me I'd better pay attention and stay, I would have gone. But no way could I have imagined this would go down. This is crazy stuff. I need some answers. Now, what's going on?" Judd lowered the binoculars and peered at him, his glare saying it all—he wanted the full story. "What happened out there? What kind of trouble are you in?"

Kirk had yet to tell him much of anything so why

was Judd already blaming him? He definitely didn't appreciate the accusation in the other man's tone.

He scraped a hand down his face. How did he keep his cover? Should he bother even trying, given the circumstances? This was Judd, after all. They'd served together and had gone through some harrowing experiences. He could trust this man with his life.

"And what about the girl?" Judd continued, without giving Kirk a chance to respond. "Cora's her name?"

"Yes. Cora."

"You two seem cozy."

"What? No. Not at all. I worked with her on the *Sea Dragon*." *That's all.*

Judd gave a knowing laugh. "Right."

Kirk ground his molars. "Look, whatever you think is going on between Cora and I isn't important right now. The truth is that someone tried to kill her today."

"You mean the explosion, the destruction of that research vessel, is because someone wants her dead?"

"Yeah. That was my reaction." Kirk filled him in on everything that had transpired that day—from finding Cora washed up on the shore, to the murder of one of the men he suspected was responsible, to the captain fleeing in the last dinghy minutes before the bombs had gone off.

Judd's dark brown eyes scrutinized Kirk as he slowly shook his head. "Man, you know how to draw trouble. After all, we called you Kirk 'Here comes trouble' Higgins for a reason. Looks like you lived up to your nickname, man, attracting real danger. Only this time someone wants to kill this chick and you find yourself as the hero in the middle. If you come out on top in this one, you deserve a new nickname." Judd's robust laugh eased some of the tension as the big guy squeezed Kirk's shoulder, then slapped him on the back. "I know you can do it."

"Thanks for your vote of confidence." *I think*. He wasn't exactly sure Judd had meant any of it as a compliment. Add to that, he didn't feel heroic at the moment, and wouldn't until he got to the bottom of this and Cora was safe.

But he had a feeling the explosion wasn't just about Cora. That it was meant to take him out, as well as to destroy evidence. Someone was on to him and they had wanted to cover their tracks, which had included murdering Trip, a player in this game.

Judd's frown deepened. He lifted the binoculars again. "Well, what do you know."

"What is it?" Kirk was eager to take a look.

With his beefy arms, Judd passed the binoculars to Kirk.

"The cavalry has arrived—a Coast Guard cutter."

"And that surprises you?"

"These waters are isolated. The nearest Coast Guard station is Port Townsend. They have their hands full with rescues and smugglers. The list goes on."

"I would think a bombed boat would be at the top of their list. We should head that way and tell them what we know. We don't want to leave the scene, but…" Kirk peered through the binoculars. A smallish cutter was headed toward the explosion site. What looked like an eighty-seven-foot marine protector patrol boat now approached what was left of the burning hulk—the parts that hadn't yet sunk in the ocean, though some pieces would probably remain floating until recovered. "I need to make a call before we head that way. Can I use your comms?"

"Sure. Use my satellite phone." Judd found it and tossed it to him. "I'll get us going while you make the call."

Kirk hoped he could get ahold of his superior. He dialed the number, then ended the call before it connected. He'd learned to listen to his gut instinct. Something in him was hesitating about calling Matt, and he remembered he'd made the decision earlier to call Commander Jackson first so called him.

Even though Kirk was breaking the chain of command, ultimately, he felt responsible to Jackson to find out what happened to his son. Matt hadn't been on board with the mission, but had had no choice after receiving his instructions from the powers that be. While he waited for the call to connect, hoping and praying he could reach Jackson without delay, he considered the words he would speak to the man. Kirk needed to be informative yet brief.

Within a minute he was connected with Jackson.

"Jackson here. What do you have for me, son?"

Everything and nothing. "Sir, we have a situation." He explained, as succinctly as possible, all the events of the last twelve hours. "A Coast Guard cutter is at the site of the explosion."

"I agree with you that it's possible someone knows you're undercover. I fear your time is limited to get to the bottom of what happened to my son. This has to be connected to his death."

"Yes, sir. I agree."

"After waiting too many months, I'm not inclined to

let these men slip away into the night when you're so close." Jackson paused.

"Sir?" What was the man saying, exactly?

"I'm giving you twenty-four hours to find Captain Menken and his connections to the murder and the destruction of the *Sea Dragon*. Leave it to me to clear it with your superior, if warranted."

"Yes, sir." Matt was going to love that.

"I'll take full responsibility for any backlash in my next instructions—do not engage with the Coast Guard. That will only delay you."

"But—"

"We could lose the leads by the time you're done. Are we clear?"

If he understood Jackson, Kirk had already wasted precious time by sitting here on this boat. He should already be tracking Menken. But he'd needed to catch his breath. Needed to save Cora and decompress.

Judd strode toward him on the deck.

"Crystal." He ended the call. *Do not engage with the Coast Guard.*

He had twenty-four hours to find answers, and in the meantime, he had to keep Cora safe. Jackson hadn't even mentioned or addressed Cora's safety, and to Kirk, her safety was *his* priority, no matter that Jackson wanted answers about his son.

Drake's troubles were over, but Cora was still alive. Kirk intended to keep her that way.

Still, getting the bad guys—those who wanted her dead—was key in securing her safety.

"Well?" Judd asked.

"Let's head to Farrow Village. We'll possibly find Menken and at least some of the crew there since that's been their hangout while the *Sea Dragon*…" He didn't bother finishing that sentence.

"What about the Coast Guard?"

"Later. I don't have time to mess with them."

Judd arched a brow. "You're working on a covert operation. I'd have to be a dummy not to figure that out."

Kirk was sure he hadn't been that obvious on the *Sea Dragon*. Just another researcher and head diver doing his job. So he wouldn't take Judd's comment personally.

"It's okay," Judd said. "You don't need to say anything. I probably shouldn't have, either. I can help if you need me."

"You've already done so much. You dragged us from the water after that explosion." Kirk eyed Judd. They'd been a team before. He might need some help to keep Cora safe until this was over. "But I appreciate your offer. I can think of a thing or two I could use your assistance with."

"It's the girl, isn't it? You want me to watch her, keep her safe, while you do your thing."

"Got a problem with that?" Kirk asked.

"It's not nearly as exciting, but sure. I'm here to help. Just one question."

"What's that?"

Judd hesitated. "What are you going to do with her when this is over?"

Kirk understood the deeper meaning of his friend's question. The guy knew him too well. Didn't mean Kirk liked the answer he gave. "We're not together like that. I'm sure we'll go our separate ways."

Just like they'd done before. Truth. The only problem with that truth was that it left him deeply disturbed when it should have had no effect on him at all.

FIVE

I don't want to die. I don't want to die.

I have to escape!

Cora sat up and gasped for breath. Sweat drenched her body. Another dream. That was all.

Or was it?

Heart still pounding, she took in her surroundings. The gentle rocking, the design of the small quarters, told her she was on a boat all right—but not the *Sea Dragon.*

Where am I?

Whose clothes am I wearing?

Oh, yeah. She was on Judd's boat. A friend of Kirk's. She was wearing Judd's too-big shirt and sweats. But at least she was warm and dry. Still, she felt utterly unsettled and struggled to recall why fear had surfaced in her thoughts. She concentrated, focused on remembering. Then…

Images accosted her. The explosion. Kirk. Being attacked by a diver. Cora pressed her face into her hands and let the sobs rack her, something she hadn't allowed herself to do until this moment. She tried to keep it quiet. Didn't want the two men to hear her. She especially didn't want Kirk to try to comfort her again—his brand of reassurance had the maddening effect of stirring memories and longings in her that she fought to ignore as it was. Still, his strong arms around her could go a long way in helping her to deal. Could she be any weaker? She couldn't give in to needing him like that.

No.

She had to be strong on her own. Why was she suddenly having these thoughts about him? Maybe this whole situation had knocked her out of balance. On the other hand, why shouldn't it?

Remember Stephan? Kirk is his brother.

There. She was in control. Kirk's nearness, his reassurance and protectiveness didn't bother her at all now.

But getting her equilibrium again where Kirk was concerned didn't do a thing for her lost footing regarding this entire situation. Trip was dead. Lance with him. People she knew and had worked with could be complicit in their deaths. The research vessel had been destroyed and, for all practical purposes, her career with it. The job she'd dreamed about. Something to actually make a difference in this world. Something that could even hold a candle to what her siblings had accomplished. What her parents had accomplished before their tragic deaths.

She rubbed her hands. *What am I thinking? People are dead!*

What did anyone's accomplishments matter in the face of death? More people could still die. What did her dream job matter in the face of danger?

When the tears were spent, she swiped them away. She wouldn't cry again until this was over. Had the Coast Guard arrived yet? She was more than ready to be off this boat and on the cutter with the Coast Guard who could deliver her home.

Then what? How did she recover from this tragedy?

She crawled from the bed and eased down to the deck. Cora leaned against the bed and pulled her knees up to her chest.

Her issues were wrapped up in much more than moving past the grief and getting on with her life. After all, this wasn't something a person could easily recover from. Someone had tried to kill her today. Subtly at first—a diving accident. Who would question that? Then they'd tried to take her out, along with a research vessel worth a kazillion dollars.

Anyone willing to do that would stop at nothing.

Cora couldn't just fade away quietly into the night. She couldn't just go home and be safe. What if whoever wanted her dead came for her there?

They wanted her dead for whatever was inside her—something she couldn't remember.

Before she could catch herself, she screamed her frustration.

The expected knock came at the door. "Cora, you okay in there?"

Kirk's concerned tone came through loud and clear. Even the sound of his voice comforted her. Yeah, she really was desperate. But she was scared, too. Terrified. "I'm fine."

"Can you open up so I can see for myself?"

His question brought on a soft chuckle. She unlocked the door and pulled it wide. His piercing blue eyes startled her.

Concern rippled through his gaze. "I heard you scream. You're not okay."

"Did you have me open the door to call me a liar?" She'd meant to tease him.

His right cheek hitched slightly. "I know you. You're trying to turn this around on me so you can avoid answering the question."

He knew her that well? "No. And there's nothing I want to talk about, Kirk. Now, what's the plan?"

She shoved past him into the tight space of the passageway, which put her entirely too close to this broad-shouldered, surfer-looking guy. Once again, she reminded herself he could be a liar like his brother, and she shouldn't trust any traitorous feelings for him that surfaced.

Shame flooded her. Would it be so wrong to give Kirk a chance to be himself? To be who he was without her thinking he might be like Stephan? Kirk's only crime, if you could call it that, was that he hadn't wanted her. He'd shoved her off on his brother. She wanted to blame him for that, but the decision to be with Stephan was really all on her.

She waited for his reply and realized he hadn't given her an answer because he was studying her. He knew she was preoccupied. She was glad he couldn't read her mind. "Are we going to meet the Coast Guard or what?"

"We're heading to the island."

"Where we'll talk to the authorities, right?"

"I don't want the people responsible to get away. I want to find them first. If we talk to the authorities, that will take too much time. Are you going to trust me on this?" His arms were crossed, and his blue gaze—so intense, so penetrating—held her captive as he waited for her answer. All she could think about was that she wanted him to grip her shoulders, pull her against him like he'd done before. But he'd backed off from touching her.

She'd already decided that she would trust him, but it was more about how far. They weren't going to talk to the authorities? How far should she go along with him? "Okay. Sure. I trust you to a point."

The slight darkening of his blue eyes told her he didn't like her answer.

"Fair enough. But…trust me in this. Give me time to track Captain Menken. I know he's responsible. We've already wasted too much time on the *Clara Steele* as it is. Menken could already be well on his way to escaping."

She had to concede he was right on that point. "If he thinks we're dead, though, he might still be on the island and talking to the Coast Guard or other authorities himself. He'll want to express his shock at the explosion and our deaths. We can't know if that diver who attacked us made it back or communicated with him."

Kirk's approving grin sent a ping of pleasure through her heart. "Well, we have a surprise for him, don't we?"

"Yes, we do. I can't wait to get to the island." She followed him back to the galley, securing the sweats that kept trying to fall right off. "I need some new clothes."

He immediately sobered. "I hadn't meant that so literally, as in, you're going with me. You're not. You're staying with Judd on the boat. He'll keep you safe. It's too dangerous."

"Oh, yeah? Did you see what happened to the *Sea Dragon*? Nowhere is safe. I'm going with you. You can't keep me here against my will."

Her hazel eyes flashed at him. Cora was much better than he was at not backing down. The woman stood up for herself, even when faced with an intimidating—or, in this case, life-and-death—situation. Something Kirk might do well to learn from. He'd backed down far too often in the past when he should have taken a stand.

And right now, Cora had taken a stand and she had a valid point. She was always making good points. That's what he lo—wait, liked—about her.

"You're not here against your will. Why would you even use a term like that? You're here so I can keep you safe. That's my priority." Another good point—she was safer here than on the island for now. "And don't worry. I'll get you some decent clothes while I'm there. Let's see…" He let his gaze take in her form, looking her up and down. "What are you, about a size six?"

Her pale features turned a nice shade of pink. "Don't worry about getting me clothes. I have more at home. I'm going with you. In fact, I'd like to catch a ferry from the island back to Seattle and be done with this." She had family she could stay with who could keep her safe. She averted her gaze as though he'd stared her down and won.

Not something he would have expected.

He lifted her chin, urging her beautiful eyes back up to his. Her gaze still flashed and sparked—good. He mustered a heartfelt, pleading look and hoped she saw and understood—something beyond what he could put into words. "You know that it's not safe until we figure this out. Give me a day, Cora. Give me until tomorrow to get information we can give to the authorities."

"Are you kidding me? I can't stay on this boat alone. I won't. I'll be safer with you. What are you afraid of?" She hesitated, her eyes seeming to search his very soul, as if she saw his wounds and flaws. "Remember, you saved my life twice already. As long as I'm with you, I'm safe."

She truly believed she was safer with him? Her confidence in him, put like that, swelled up inside and all the dark places inside him lit up. Was she putting too much trust in him?

Her soft brown hair had dried now and framed her face. Her green-flecked eyes glistened, imploring him to let her go with him, though he knew that if Cora really wanted off this boat, nothing he could say would keep her here. So he suspected that she wanted him to validate her decision to leave. Hmm. She'd always been much too serious and guarded, but now she appeared vulnerable—wanting his approval.

Could it be that Cora wanted him to *want* her to go? That she wanted Kirk to want her with him?

And he definitely wanted her with him. Sure. More than he should. In a way he shouldn't. And certainly not like this. Not under these circumstances. But he couldn't tell her any of that. Regardless, his heart bounced in a hundred directions against his rib cage.

He fisted his hands to get control of his emotions. This was definitely not the time to be ruled by them. But when it came to Cora, he couldn't seem to help himself. Once again, he regretted ever introducing her to his brother because that had given her the opportunity to choose Stephan.

He'd taken too long to respond and she took that as his reply—a big fat no.

She stepped away and sighed. "I'm going to the island, Kirk, with or without your approval."

Figured. "All right, Cora. But if you're coming with me then Judd needs to come, too, in case I need to engage Captain Menken. I need Judd's help in keeping you safe if things turn south. You know how bad it can get. You've seen it for yourself and nearly been the victim of it twice now."

"I didn't mean for you to think that keeping me safe is your responsibility, only that I'm safer with you than I would be here on the boat without you. Besides, I want to face Captain Menken, too." She gritted her teeth, as if she could hardly contain her anger. "Do you think he killed Trip before he left? I have to wonder if he did something to Lance, too, and he was already dead in his stateroom or somewhere else on the boat before the explosions and that's why he didn't meet us at the stern."

Tears pooled in her eyes but they didn't spill over. If even one tear had slid down her cheek he would have been quick to wipe it away. But Cora wouldn't give him the chance. Instead, she stood taller and sucked in a long breath as if to say something.

But Kirk beat her to it. "I don't know. But I intend to find out."

Needing to sever this pull she had on him, he turned away from her. Time to get back on task.

She followed Kirk up to the helm. Judd steered them toward Farrow Island, which would be hopping with tourists this time of year for the annual Tour de Farrow, where people would bike all over the sprawling island, through the national park and temperate rain forests.

And in a few short moments the *Clara Steele* would reach the island.

Tension corded his muscles.

If Menken had already talked to the authorities and

claimed that Lance, Kirk and Cora had died in the explosion, and then Kirk and Cora showed up alive, blame could be cast on them, depending on the story Menken told. Then he and Cora could be suspected of murder and possibly even taken into custody, at least until the truth came out. That would mean she would be exposed and vulnerable to those who would kill her.

A beefy hand gripped his arm, startling him. "Snap out of it, man. It's going to be okay."

"I was that obvious, huh?"

"Yep. You need to focus."

Yeah, he was probably running too many paranoid scenarios through his mind, but given what they had been through today, maybe not. Cora stood at the rail, the wind blowing through her short brown tresses. He wanted to pull her close and protect her forever, a feeling he should definitely not have at this moment. He wouldn't let himself get tangled up with her again. Not after what happened. But more importantly, those thoughts were a distraction to his multiple missions—

Protect Cora.

Find answers.

Stop those responsible for murder and Drake's disappearance.

From the moment he had learned that Cora was on the *Sea Dragon*, Kirk had feared this very thing. He had hoped his foreboding had been nothing more than paranoia and worst-case imaginings. But the worst had happened and they were in the middle of it now.

God, why did this have to happen? Why Cora? Please help me to keep her safe. Help me to find the men responsible.

"Cora." He said her name so softly, he wondered that she could hear him over the wind.

Slowly she turned her head, her gaze meeting his.

"Do you remember anything yet?"

Her lips pressed into a thin line as she shook her head. Knowing what she had seen or overheard but couldn't remember would go a long way in solving this mystery. It had to be linked to what he'd discovered on Trip's computer. He suspected it could be as simple as her having stumbled across, her witnessing something going down, which made her a liability.

Should Kirk tell her about his discovery? That could jog her memory. He struggled with holding back everything he knew. But right now, he couldn't trust his own judgment when he was near her. Best to wait until he was sure.

His thoughts scattered as Judd steered the *Clara Steele* into a slip at the small island marina. Once the boat was moored, Kirk jumped to the pier and glanced up at Cora.

He had no idea who or what he would face on Farrow Island, but even from here, he could hear a crowd. He remembered there was another event going on besides the biking, but he couldn't remember what.

Was letting her come a mistake? Foreboding grew in his gut. How had he let her convince him this was a good idea? She'd insisted she would leave with him no matter what he thought, but he could have tried harder to get her to stay.

Judd hopped onto the boardwalk. "What are you waiting for?"

Cora followed Judd's lead.

"I don't have a good feeling about this," Kirk said.

"We talked about this already, Kirk. Besides, you really can't stop me."

"What do you want to do first?" Judd eyed the marina, wariness in his eyes.

Kirk had less than twenty-four hours to find Captain Menken and anyone involved in his schemes. To get justice for Drake. If Cora wasn't with him, he would already be tracking down Menken and anyone else belonging to the crew. He'd just brought her into the lion's den—all because he wanted to please her? That he'd let her convince him that he was some hero? Some protector?

But it was too late to stop her. She and Judd were already making their way toward the town in search of the *Sea Dragon* crew. He sighed. Best to get this over with—get the information he needed back to Commander Jackson, and then the authorities, before the bad guys closed in on them.

Everything seemed so bleak at the moment. Except, well…there was some good news. This was such a beautiful day, and with plenty of tourists taking over the island, they could blend in and maybe even go undetected by Menken and Coburn.

With Cora strolling between him and Judd, they left the marina and entered the quaint, historic Farrow Village on a side street—no one would ever guess that a murderer, maybe even more than one, walked among these people made up of farmers, fishermen, telecommuters and tourists.

Kirk and Cora found a T-shirt shop where they bought some new clothes, including shorts. At least the time spent in the store allowed them to engage people about what was going on.

Most people talked about the biking tour of the island, the bands or the fireworks planned.

Less than three hours had passed since the research vessel had been taken out. If anyone on the island had heard or seen the explosion, or if news had traveled of the sunken research vessel, no one spoke of it.

"Where do you think the crew members would go?" Judd asked.

"They would have picked up the part for the ROV," Cora said. "And then they would have gathered supplies. They would have found Shari to bring her back, too. I know some of them went to Seattle for the couple of days it would take for Trip and Lance to fix the ROV." Her brow furrowed with concern. "But Coburn and Shari and whoever was with them would have already headed back to the *Sea Dragon* so they must know it has sunk, either because they tried to find it or because they were complicit in the explosion."

"Maybe. In that case they might be talking to the Coast Guard or the police, unless they were involved in the explosion, like you said. Then they could already have left the island." Kirk watched for danger as he and Judd both flanked Cora. Judd had his back, he knew that, and was glad for the man's help.

Kirk owed him, that was for sure.

"And if they weren't part of it, and they didn't know yet, then they would probably be at that bar, Jed's Drink and Eats, before heading back to the *Sea Dragon*." Cora pointed at the door of a slim structure positioned between two bigger buildings—a bank and a bike shop.

Somewhere, the cacophonous racket of firecrackers went off in celebration of the events of the weekend.

But Kirk didn't miss the splintering of wood near Cora's head on the wall behind her.

"Get down!"

SIX

Because she was on edge already, the firecrackers startled her.

Kirk had forced her to the ground. His muscles tense, he hovered over her, protectiveness radiating from him. The fireworks must have startled him, too. That's all it was, wasn't it? Fireworks? Still, her heart hadn't stopped pounding.

People passed and stared at them like they were crazy—well, maybe more out of curiosity. Kirk pulled her to her feet and quickly ushered her around the corner, then into a crouching position.

"It's only the fireworks, dude," Judd said, though he stood in a defensive posture—a shield to protect the both of them. "Relax."

Had Kirk been overreacting?

Cora tried to stand and escape her human body armor.

"No." He gripped her arm and kept her huddled against the bike shop wall. "Please stay down."

His bulging biceps told her well enough she couldn't escape his raw strength if she wanted to. And she *definitely* wanted to escape. Kirk's presence. This island. This entire scenario. But not before she looked Captain

Menken in the eyes. Still, she should appreciate that Kirk continued to keep her alive.

She'd wanted to be near him, knowing he could keep her safe, but enough was enough. For crying out loud, she could just go to the authorities here on the island, except for Kirk and his concern about who they could trust. He wasn't completely wrong there.

"This is ridiculous!" Cora made to stand again, fury boiling inside. He peered down at her, shadows framing the edges of his face and emphasizing his piercing eyes. What she saw in his gaze kept her frozen in place. Yeah, he could definitely kill with one look. Or, in this case, turn her completely immobile.

"Someone took a shot at you. The wood splintered next to your head. Didn't you even notice?"

Her knees trembled. She struggled to speak. "What? Are you sure?"

"I'm dead certain."

"Come on, then," Judd said, leading the way.

Kirk's hand still gripping her arm, he kept Cora close as they blended into the crowd. If someone was taking shots at her, at them, how had that someone thought they could take her out with all these people around? Or maybe they didn't care, and in that case, wouldn't Cora's and Kirk's presence in the middle of this throng put all these folks in danger?

"Where are we going?" she asked.

"We could follow these people to the main event where the music is coming from. Listen to the bands and watch the fireworks, but it's all an act, of course," Judd said.

"We could get some bikes and ride out of here, but I think Judd's right. We'll flow with the tourists and then slip into Jed's bar to see if we can find Menken or Coburn or anyone at all related to the *Sea Dragon*."

"Except…are you sure your crewmates aren't heading over to watch the show?" Judd asked.

Too much was happening too fast. She didn't know the answers when she should. Cora had to think on her feet, as the saying went. Her mind was still scrambling to catch up with this latest turn of events.

Kirk led them back into a shadowed corner next to the bike shop. He guarded her and watched the passing crowd as he urged them into the shadows. Then he turned to face the both of them.

"No. We're not going to the big event, whatever it is. We're not getting stuck in the crowd. In fact, I'm the only one staying on this island. Menken, or whoever is behind this, obviously knows we survived. Cora's life is in danger. I need you to get her back to the *Clara Steele* and take the boat out somewhere safe. Keep Cora safe for me."

Kirk grabbed Judd's hand. The two men appeared to have an understanding and their agreement had nothing at all to do with asking Cora her opinion.

"Don't I have a say in this?" She crossed her arms.

"Sure you do." Kirk towered over her and leaned in entirely too close. "What would you like to say?"

His question surprised her. She'd prepared to make a stand. To do battle. Maybe she still would have to do that once she gave him her reply. "I want to find out who tried to kill us. I would like to see Captain Menken myself. Face off with him."

"I know what you want. We're all after the same thing. But right now can you honestly tell me you believe it's in your best interest to stay on the island? Can you tell me you think that if you stay, and my attention and focus is on keeping you safe, that we'll reach our goal?"

He had her there. "I…I hadn't thought of it that way. But it's more than that, Kirk. I must know something they want. I can help. Somehow I can help you, I know it."

His expression softened. "Then help me this way. Go back with Judd, just until I find out who is behind this and who we can trust. I'll come back for you and we can make more plans, but plans that don't include putting you in the line of fire. Do you trust me?"

How many times would he ask her that? Until she gave him the right response? She stared into his blue gaze far longer than she should. She wasn't sure she could take this man's intense focus on her much longer, but she refused to turn away. "You know I do."

Relief washed across his features. "Then trust me when I say this is the fastest way to find Menken—me on my own while I know you're safe. We tried it your way and it didn't work."

She nodded. "Okay, then. But I don't want you to be in the line of fire, either. Why should you be the one to do this? Because you're the big strong man?" *Way to go, Cora.* He was a hero. Had she already forgotten that he'd saved her? His quick thinking meant he had found and revived her after the diving accident. And he had gotten them off that boat today before it was too late.

"Because—" He stopped before finishing. Catching himself. An emotion she couldn't read surged in his gaze. Deception? No, that couldn't be it. She was reading him wrong. It was just because of Stephan that she'd ever doubted Kirk. She hoped she wasn't making a mistake in trusting him.

"I'm sorry. I didn't mean it that way."

"No problem. I won't hold you captive, Cora. You're free to walk this out on your own." He stepped back, his gesture confirming his words, but his jaw worked back and forth.

She suspected that he hoped she wouldn't take him up on going it alone. She would be a fool to do it. At least she knew that much. "I know you were in the navy. You're skilled and up to the task. I can use a weapon like the average person, and that's about it. I'm better with a speargun."

His cheek hitched. Phew. They were good again. Strange how much she hated for him to be upset with her.

"I'm scared for you, that's all." And she meant it.

"You don't need to be."

"We're wasting time." Judd had hovered near the edge of their hiding corner. "Whoever shot at her before will catch up if we don't hurry."

Kirk drew near again, as though...as though he might kiss her. "I'm glad you're seeing reason. Now, let's get you back to safety."

Where she should have stayed. She had only cost Kirk time by insisting she come with them. But she hadn't known someone would try to kill her. Someone who must be keeping very close tabs on her whereabouts.

A bullet whizzed by her cheek. Cora screamed.

Kirk and Judd covered her and hurried her away from the crowd, through shops and between buildings, back to the pier. Her mind and heart raced, believing at any moment she could be standing in the presence of her Maker.

Kirk tugged her into the shadows. The marina was packed with boats, the *Clara Steele* mere yards away. "Judd is going to check his boat before you board to make sure it wasn't rigged with explosives while we were out."

"He's risking his life for us," she said.

"We learn to do that serving in the armed forces, and that skill, that propensity to be on guard, never really goes away." His blue-eyed gaze peered down at her, and that intense feeling swept over her again—that Kirk would kiss her. And to her utter disbelief she wanted that kiss. Her attraction for him had never gone away, even though she'd tried repeatedly to tamp it down. She'd already been hurt by this guy and she wouldn't give him the chance to hurt her again.

Judd's signal interrupted what might have been a goodbye-and-keep-safe kiss. She should have been relieved rather than disappointed.

Kirk ushered her to the *Clara Steele*. Judd had already prepared to leave the dock, and it looked like Kirk would hang back and pick off anyone who tried to harm her. Maybe in subduing the shooter, he could get answers.

"Keep safe, Cora," he said as she boarded the boat.

"Stay alive," she said. "Find who did this. I know you won't disappoint me."

A bullet slammed into the *Clara Steele*, much too near her head.

Cora's in danger!

Gunfire rang out around him—and Cora was the target. The marina was relatively deserted, with most people touring the village, the countryside or attending the main event. Anyone at the marina might have thought the sounds were firecrackers—but Kirk would never have been fooled.

Pulse racing, he returned fire, aiming at the stack of crates from where shots were fired, giving Cora the chance to slip belowdecks as Judd maneuvered and steered the *Clara Steele* out of the marina.

Faster, Judd. Move faster! Kirk willed his buddy to push the trawler, but the boat couldn't so quickly escape. That's why it was up to Kirk to hold off whoever wanted Cora dead. Was it Coburn or Menken shooting at them? Or both? Who else of the twenty crew members was involved? He suspected it boiled down to a handful or fewer and he already had at least two suspects.

As the *Clara Steele* fled the gunfire, Kirk thought about his decision to send her away. He hoped he'd made the right one. He wasn't entirely sure Cora would be safer out there on the water after what they'd already been through over the last twelve hours.

After all, this had started out on the water in the Salish Sea.

But Judd knew what he was doing. He claimed he had practice at finding the best secluded spots to fish—nobody would be able to find them.

Slinking between boats moored in their slips, Kirk made his way toward the stack of wooden slatted crates from behind which the shots had been fired. He slipped up next to a crate, held his weapon at the ready and crept around. Ready to shoot each time he turned a corner.

But the shooter was long gone.

Looked like his own bullets marred the surface of a couple of crates. He remained next to them and let his gaze roam the marina and then Farrow Village, bustling with activity. In the distance beyond the marina, houses with green grass in the yards lined the beach. Gentle waves rolled onto the gray, pebbled shore. Seagulls searched for food—crabs or old french fries, take your pick.

Though Kirk wouldn't consider Farrow Island large—fourteen miles long and fifty-four miles of shoreline—it wasn't exactly something he could explore in a day. Still, he would find those responsible. Somehow. Someway. Of course, they could very well flee the island, and then what? But Kirk had a feeling the bad guys would stick close enough to make sure all loose ends were tied up.

Cora was a loose end.

As he made his way back to Farrow Village, he headed to Jed's, the restaurant and bar where he knew at least one person from the *Sea Dragon* would be hanging out. He mentally ran through the list of crew members again. Were any of them the shooter? He honestly couldn't picture the men he'd worked with on the *Sea Dragon* for the last couple of months taking shots at Cora. They all seemed to adore her. Especially Lance, who'd clearly had a thing for her—but he'd died on the *Sea Dragon*, his body lost forever along with Trip's. Nor could Kirk picture the jovial Captain Menken being responsible for the bombs that had taken out the research vessel, his intent to get rid of the evidence and loose ends—to kill Cora and Trip. But the guilty parties often had others fooled.

Perhaps Lance and Kirk would simply have been collateral damage.

Allowing outrage to fuel his focus, he blended into the crowd again, aware that he would be the target now, at least on this island. If it hadn't been for the series of unfortunate events—Cora seeing what she shouldn't have seen and then Kirk's cover somehow being blown—they might still be on the *Sea Dragon*.

Then again, this could all be on Trip.

Across the street and a couple of storefronts down, Jed's was open for business. The sense of urgency that lives depended on him finding the killers before someone else was murdered accosted him. That, and the fact that Jackson had given him a set time to solve this.

Kirk dug down deep and sent up a silent prayer. *Lord, please let me find someone here. I need answers and I need them fast.*

He stood back in the shadows until his eyes adjusted to the dim lighting typical in this kind of establishment. A woman in conversation with a couple of guys at a table laughed. Her voice carried over to Kirk. "You'd be disappointed," she said.

Her pronouncement brought back Cora's last words to him.

I know you won't disappoint me.

And that was just it, wasn't it? Kirk had disappointed his family already. He was a walking disappointment. His father had made that exceedingly clear when Kirk hadn't become an attorney and part of the family business—Higgins and Sons, Attorneys at Law.

If he didn't find out who was responsible in the next few hours, he'd not only let down Drake and Commander Jackson, but also Matt, his supervisor. He'd chosen this career; the least he could do was succeed in it. Secure justice. And maybe, in getting justice for those who were killed, he wouldn't let Cora down, either.

A familiar guffaw from the bar pulled his focus back. The hair on the back of his neck stood on end.

Coburn. Declan Coburn was a retired Alaskan Airlines pilot turned shipwreck diver and maritime historian—but mostly he worked security on the *Sea Dragon*. A lot of good that had done. The guy also loved to drink. He couldn't drink before a dive, but he hit the bars every chance he got.

Kirk slowly approached, fully aware that Coburn's reaction to seeing him alive and well could tell him everything. He slid onto a stool at the bar right next to Coburn and ordered a sparkling water with lime.

Coburn's eyes narrowed slightly. "Hey…hey, man. I thought you were back at the *Sea Dragon*." His gaze searched the room. For a quick escape? "What? Did you decide to hit the island for the fireworks later?"

He knows something, all right.

"Nah. I just came to look for you guys. I was waiting on the *Sea Dragon* for you to bring Shari back for Cora. Remember? I thought there might be some sort of holdup." More than anything, Kirk wanted to pound this man for what he'd done to Cora. To find out what had happened on that dive this morning that had left her for dead, and so much more. "Did you find Shari? When was the rest of the crew planning to head back with the part for the ROV?"

"Uh… I don't know. I wasn't the one in charge of that. But I had planned to join everyone in a couple of hours, probably." Coburn eased off his stool and downed the rest of his liquor. He gripped the edge of the bar.

The fact that he was half drunk could help Kirk find out what he needed.

"I need to find the restroom," Coburn said.

"You're not going anywhere." Kirk downed his seltzer water, then slammed the glass on the bar much too hard.

"What do you mean, man? I have to go."

When Coburn moved, Kirk grabbed his arm and twisted it behind his back, pressing the muzzle of his gun into his side. "Keep quiet. You're coming with me."

He ushered Coburn out of the bar, aware the man could try to make his escape there. He was physically fit—despite his love affair with alcohol—and fully capable of taking Kirk out if he got the advantage. Except today it was unlikely he would get that advantage since he'd had too much to drink. Kirk forced him between the buildings.

Even with one arm twisted behind his back, Coburn somehow managed to pull a knife from his jeans pocket.

With no one in the alley to interfere, Kirk pointed his weapon at Coburn so he could look down the barrel instead of only feeling it in his side. Maybe that would be much more intimidating. "Come on. You're not actually going to try to fight me."

The man flicked the knife at him. Kirk jerked out of the way, but he wasn't nearly quick enough. The knife sliced through his upper arm near the previous wound and seared him with pain. But even worse, Coburn took advantage of the momentary distraction and took off, running out of the alley and around the corner.

The man had called Kirk's bluff—he wasn't prepared to kill Coburn, especially since he hadn't gotten the information he needed. Kirk put the weapon away and prepared to follow.

He could easily catch up with the drunk man.

Kirk fled the alley and turned right, the same direction Coburn had taken. He spotted the man, caught up between two other crew members—engineer Scott Epperson and computer tech Chuck Hays.

Even better. Kirk stepped back into the shadows. He could follow. Watch and listen. Find out what he needed to know.

"You drunk again?" Hays asked. "You were supposed to be at the marina two hours ago!"

"You stupid jerk!" Epperson looked like he wanted to pummel Coburn but held back. "They're here on the island. They're alive."

"I know that." Coburn pulled away and stumbled into the wall.

Kirk wasn't far behind. All they had to do was look over their shoulders.

"What do you know? You know nothing. What little you do know—like when to meet us and where—you can't even follow through." Hays punched him.

"I know the code."

Seething, Hays yanked Coburn to him by the collar. "Quiet. Do you want to get us killed?"

Coburn laughed almost hysterically, as if fear had taken hold but he didn't care. "You mean like Lance killed Trip? Tried to kill Cora?" He wiped his eyes, crying now.

Lance murdered Trip? Lance was behind the attempt on Cora's life? Kirk's mind stumbled at the news.

"Sweet Cora," Coburn continued. "Well, you don't

have to worry anymore. Verone has her. He'll keep her for us."

Verone…

Judd Verone.

Kirk stumbled back into the shadows. He'd trusted the wrong person.

He'd left Cora with that murderous traitor.

SEVEN

In the *Clara Steele*'s galley, Cora couldn't stop pacing. "What if something happens to him? How will we know? Maybe this wasn't a good idea. Why aren't we going to the police again?"

Judd chuckled. "I can only answer one question at a time. You don't need to worry. Kirk knows how to handle himself. He won't let us down." Judd stood at the counter waiting for teabags to steep in a mug of hot water. "I'm sure he will contact the appropriate authorities, too. But right now, we have to keep you safe. All you need to do is relax and trust Kirk to know what to do."

"I know. I trust him. But I can't help but worry about him. I can't help but worry about us. Look what already happened. What if they followed us here? Shouldn't we be keeping watch on deck?"

"Nobody followed us. Even if they were to search, they couldn't find us in this cove. This is one of my favorite places to fish. An out-of-the-way spot not frequented by tourists or fishermen. Your man trusted me to keep you safe and that's what I'm going to do."

Your man...

Right. "He's not—"

"Your man?"

"No. It's not like that." Regret curdled in her stomach over what might have been between her and Kirk.

Why had she been so quick to let Stephan charm her? Maybe it all went back to that one defining moment. The moment she'd *allowed* to determine how she looked at herself.

Her date to the prom—Jimmy McElroy—had dumped her off on another guy so he could leave with a girl he liked better than Cora. If she was honest, she'd felt a little like Kirk had done the same thing. He'd let Stephan charm her and pretty much take over. She'd wanted Kirk to step up and claim her, so that's why she'd stood there and waited for him to act. But he hadn't. Instead he'd left.

That had hurt her more than she'd been willing to admit at the time. She'd refused to give in to that pain—to a repeat of the past—and allowed Stephan to sweep her off her feet, as it were. He seemed to want her, and she'd *needed* to be wanted. In the end, Stephan had pretended that Cora was the only one for him, but he'd been seeing another woman on the side. Of all the nerve! Why did this keep happening to her?

He was a liar. A big fat liar. Lied to her face about it on multiple occasions.

But she was the bigger liar. She had lied to herself. She had never really wanted Stephan.

It had always been Kirk. Still, it wasn't that way between them now, despite what Judd thought he knew.

"I see the way he looks at you. He cares about you like that." Judd set the mug of tea in front of her.

"For me?"

"Chamomile tea. It'll settle your nerves."

"I'm surprised a guy like you even has tea on the boat." She wrapped her hands around the mug to warm them. Drew in the light scent. Judd was more thoughtful than she could have imagined. He knew exactly what she needed right now. Could he also know what Kirk felt about Cora? "I think you're wrong about Kirk liking me. But it doesn't matter anyway."

Judd had to be wrong about Kirk. Besides, she wouldn't put herself out there to be rejected again. Kirk had already let her down in that regard once. He hadn't wanted her. And on the off chance that she and Kirk actually had a chance to try again, she was too afraid to fall in love. She'd only be lied to again. She didn't want to feel like she always had to be looking for the cracks in his veneer to see if he was lying.

"Well, I'll leave you to your thoughts," Judd said. "I think I'll go up top and make sure we're still alone in the cove, after all."

"Sure. Okay. I think I'll drink my tea and lie down. Take one of the staterooms, if that's okay."

"That's a great idea. I'll wake you when I hear from Kirk if you're not already awake."

She nodded. He disappeared up the steps, his big boots clomping as he went—to go make sure they were still alone? He'd told her all that stuff about being safe here in his favorite fishing spot, even though he couldn't be a hundred percent sure they wouldn't be discovered. She hoped they were still alone. Cora needed some downtime. She needed to catch her breath.

She brought the mug to her lips. Too hot. She set it down again.

He'd made her chamomile tea. He probably wasn't the only tough former military man who stocked chamomile tea. What a thoughtful guy. And that was just it—this didn't fit him all that well. Thoughtful, yes. Tea. No. She'd gotten a glimpse of what was inside his kitchen cabinet and hadn't seen tea.

She wished she could have stayed with Kirk. Concern for him bombarded her. Admittedly, she was terrified to be on this boat without her protector. Even Judd, with all his large size and muscles, didn't give her that sense of protection that poured off Kirk.

To his credit, the big man had tried to calm her by telling her stories of his navy adventures with Kirk.

With her cup of tea, she headed back to the stateroom she'd used earlier. For all practical purposes, Judd was a stranger to her, but he'd extended a helping hand in a dangerous situation to his navy buddy, Kirk. That should be good enough for her.

Settling on the small bed, she placed the tea on the side table and pulled a quilt decorated with anchors over her shoulders and tried to rest. Doubt held her captive, though. Who could she really trust? Who could she believe? If the men she'd worked with for six months could be murderers, then what did Cora really know about anyone? What did she know about Kirk? How did she know he wasn't involved with the murder and destruction of the boat? He'd escaped before the vessel was destroyed.

How convenient. And Kirk believed she knew something, had seen something while diving. Maybe this whole thing was a ruse on his part to learn what she knew. Except why not kill her? Unless he needed the information stuck in her mind.

Information she couldn't get herself.

Her doubts sounded over-the-top. How weird that

now that he was gone, she had once again begun to feel uncertain about where Kirk's loyalties lay. Was she so enamored with him—and she might as well add that she was, just a little—that she couldn't think straight when near him? If that was the case, she could be seriously wrong about him. Perhaps deadly wrong.

Stop it. Just stop it.

Kirk was a good guy. There was no way he was part of it. He wouldn't have saved her. She had already decided she could trust him.

Since she was unable to take a nap, maybe she should go above deck to get some fresh air and help Judd watch for danger. She cracked the stateroom door and heard his voice in the galley.

"I have her. I put a little something in her tea so she'll sleep. I'll bring her to you."

At his words, her pulse soared. Pounded in her ears so she couldn't hear anything else he said.

What did they want with her?

Someone had tried to kill her repeatedly, and now Judd was taking her to someone, against her will, thinking she was drugged and unconscious. Who were these people after her? It seemed like two different parties were at work here. Where did Judd plan to take her, and to whom?

Nausea roiled in her stomach and Cora never got seasick. She pressed her back against the wall, trying to come up with a plan of escape, but where could she go in the isolated cove if no one knew about it? She couldn't even get help. Judd would find her.

He couldn't be talking to Kirk on that phone or taking her to Kirk. That didn't make sense. He was a good guy, anyway, and the only person she could trust. All her ridiculous ruminations about trusting Kirk fell away as she faced this new threat.

Her stomach felt as though it might heave at any moment. She slowly shut the door and quietly locked it, hoping he didn't realize she had never actually drunk from the cup—it had been much too hot and she'd gotten into bed without tasting it, only to lie there, too wired with anxiety to sleep.

What should she do? *Oh, God, I'm in danger. I'm in trouble. Help me!*

Judd was huge. She had no chance of escaping him if he caught her. *Think, Cora. Think.*

How could she get away from him? Somehow, she had to escape and make it back to Farrow Island to warn Kirk not to trust the man. He'd trusted Judd implicitly.

Her elbow knocked into the lamp in the corner and it hit the floor, crashing louder than she would have expected. She flinched.

Oh, boy. She'd just alerted him to come and check on her.

A soft knock sounded at the door.

"You okay in there?" Judd's voice was low. Almost a whisper. He was assessing her current state—asleep or awake.

What should I do? What should I do?

If she'd drunk the tea, then he would expect her to be asleep and unable to respond, so she went with that. She waited to see if he would ask more questions, but she hoped he would go away, believing her asleep.

It sounded as if he quietly unlocked the door with a key. How dare he!

Still. She was in trouble now—she couldn't get back into that bed quickly enough—so she would have to pretend she'd just woken up. A glance in the mirror told her she wouldn't be able to pretend that she hadn't heard his conversation. She searched for a weapon. Anything. She wished she had a speargun—*that* she could definitely handle and maybe even win the coming battle.

Her gaze fell on the lamp she'd knocked over. It would have to do.

He slowly opened the door. At the moment he must have realized she wasn't in her bed, he opened it wider.

Now!

Putting all the force her diver muscles could muster behind it, Cora slammed the lamp into his temple. Taking the big man down required all her strength.

It was her life or his.

He slumped over onto the bed.

Tension corded her muscles. Nausea invaded her stomach again.

Was he…was he dead?

She'd prefer it if he were unconscious and not dead. She checked his pulse. Still there and beating strong.

Though Cora was much better with a speargun when it came to weapons, apparently she was also good with lamps. But right now, she had a different issue—securing Judd so he couldn't break free once he woke up. She had no way of knowing how long he would remain unconscious, so she had to work quickly.

Cora was grateful she knew how to tie knots worthy of sailors. Grabbing marine rope from the deck, she tied Judd up so that he couldn't escape without the assistance of someone with a sharp knife.

Then she made her way to the helm. Out in the open under the blue sky, she breathed in the fresh saltwater air. She was free but she wouldn't stay that way unless she got back to the island—and then what, she wasn't sure. The boat sat idling already. The anchor had already been pulled up. Good. All she had to do was steer the *Clara Steele* back to the island using the coordinates on the navigation display. She knew her way around this part of the world, though she wasn't familiar with this particular secret cove where Judd had kept her.

Lord, help me make it to Kirk. Help us figure this out. Find justice for those murdered and find safety.

Help us find our way...back to each other?

But that might be asking too much. They'd need to find each other to begin with.

No time to worry about that.

Taking the boat back to the island, she steered into a different slip from where the *Clara Steele* had docked before. For all she knew, whoever Judd had planned to hand her over to was expecting him. Watching and waiting.

Her palms slicked. Maybe it had been a bad idea to come back to Farrow Island. But Kirk was here. She had to warn him about Judd.

Not to mention someone had tried to kill her while on this island. How did she stay alive? How did she contact Kirk? She had no answers, but what she did know was that she had to get off this boat. She crept below and peeked into the stateroom where she'd left Judd tied up. She'd duct-taped his mouth so he couldn't shout threats at her and unnerve her.

"What happened to the nice man who made me tea?" She made sure he heard the sarcasm in her voice. "And, oh, by the way, I know you drugged the tea."

His glare at her spoke volumes. He would kill her when he got free.

She closed the door. Maybe she shouldn't have taunted him. She rushed to the master stateroom where Judd slept and went in. She grabbed the satellite phone. Spotted a laptop resting on the bed and snatched it up. Maybe she could find the answers to their questions. The reason for the *Sea Dragon*'s demise and all that had gone wrong. If not, then she had just stolen a computer, but she was absolutely certain the man was guilty and her life was forfeit if he got his hands on her. She wouldn't sweat the small stuff when Kirk's life was at risk.

Hers, too.

She stuffed the items in a backpack and hefted it over her shoulder.

Staying vigilant, keeping on guard to the danger around her, she hopped onto the pier and moored the *Clara Steele*. She had absolutely no idea where she was going or where Kirk could be, so she just kept walking. Found her way into the busy village. By now he would have discovered something, wouldn't he?

Had he already tried to contact Judd? To find her? She stared at the phone. Kirk wasn't going to call this, was he? And, in the meantime, this phone could be tracked. She was all but leading the killers to herself. She dropped it, stomped on it, then threw the pieces into the trash.

Worry and fear slithered around her insides and squeezed.

The most important thing she could do to help their cause was to get on Judd's laptop and see what she could find. And then she had to get off this island.

Cora made her way to the ferry terminal and booked a ride to Seattle. Once there, she could rent a car or call for backup. Her sister Jonna used to be a special agent with Homeland Security Investigations, and her husband was a former Diplomatic Security Service agent, the law enforcement of the State Department. Jonna and Ian could come and get her. Or she could contact her sister Sadie, who was married to an agent with CGIS—the Coast Guard Investigative Service. She could call someone and ask for them to pick her up. That might be safer. They would help her know what to do next.

Her ferry passage booked, she found a small internet café next to the terminal. Inside, she claimed the far corner where she could face the door. She made a note of all the exits like she had experience in finding a quick escape. At least she was learning.

Once seated, she drew in a breath. Her pulse raced erratically. *Oh, Kirk, where are you?*

Was he okay? Or had the killers gotten the best of him? All she knew to do was to help him the only way she could at the moment. Gain access to Judd's computer.

Fortunately for her, Judd wasn't using a facial recognition log-in.

Unfortunately for Judd, Cora had a great memory—except the clouded ones hidden behind the retrograde amnesia—and her years of attention to details served her well. She had watched Judd log in to his computer. She could see the keystrokes in her mind's eye. Four numbers for quick access. She had to try a few times to get the order correct, but she made it in.

Success!

She likely had limited time to browse. If Judd had escaped or someone had found and freed him, he might have software that could find the laptop or even remotely lock it and delete files. She was working on borrowed time already.

Judd had precious few files on his laptop. He had email but it was web based and she couldn't open that, but she was able to look through files in a spreadsheet program. Nothing jumped out at her. And why would it? She wasn't a computer whiz, per se, but she knew enough to be dangerous.

A strange triangular symbol caught her attention.

Dizziness swept over her. An ache stabbed through her brain.

She'd seen that before.

Memories flooded her mind.

She'd surprised Coburn and Trip on their dive. She hadn't even remembered being suspicious—that had all left her mind.

They had been perusing a gray box.

Seeing her, their eyes had grown wide. But someone from behind had cut her regulator hose and held her.

She'd fought. Twisted and turned and tried to stab whoever was holding her with her own knife. She'd escaped and swum away. Still, she'd had limited breath.

Then…nothing. She remembered nothing after that.

Tears surged in her eyes but she didn't let herself cry.

Trip and Coburn were part of this? Or had they been equally surprised by the man who'd thought he'd killed her? If so, they had told no one on the *Sea Dragon*, and then Trip had surfaced without her only to be murdered later. Once again the betrayal lambasted her.

Lord, what is going on?

Chills crawled over her. She had to get out of here.

What had she been thinking, to remain even one second longer? The ferry wouldn't leave for another two hours. Maybe she could hire a private boat. She shut the computer and was about to leave the table when a man slid into the seat across from her.

She gulped for air as her mind wrapped around what she was seeing.

Lance?

"Oh, Lance!" He was alive. Relief flooded through her. "I thought you'd died in the explosion!"

She reached across the table and grabbed his hand. Then slowly pulled her hand free. What was she thinking? She'd been so relieved to see him alive she hadn't considered what that could mean. Sure, they'd thought he died, but he hadn't. He'd survived. Did that mean he was in on it?

He leaned in and kept his voice low. "We don't have time. You're in danger. We have to get out of here."

"What do you know about it?"

Lance's gaze swept the small café. "We can't talk here."

How had he found her?

"I'm not going anywhere with you. I have to find Kirk."

"No. Kirk… He rigged the *Sea Dragon* to blow up. He's using you, Cora."

"Using me for what?"

"Can we get out of here?" He rose and held his hand out.

"You're wrong about him."

"Then you can prove that to me. But let's get somewhere safe and then we can figure out who to trust."

She fled the café with Lance, who led her over to a small sedan.

Cora hesitated. Backed away. "I can't go with you."

"Look, I can take you wherever you need to go, but I'm worried. Someone tried to kill me. They tried to kill us all out there. Don't you realize how much danger you're in?"

"Did you go to the police?"

"Yes. I told them everything. But they can't keep me safe. They only have so much manpower this weekend. They called the Coast Guard to investigate. While I was waiting at the police station someone tried to kill me, so I can't wait around."

Even so... "You're wrong about Kirk."

"Fine." Lance stepped closer. He jabbed something into her side. "Now, just get in the car. You run, you're dead."

They climbed into the car and Lance pointed the weapon at her. "This is for your own protection, Cora. Since you don't believe that I'm only trying to help."

Cora had had enough. He disgusted her!

"Please don't look at me like that," he said.

"Like what? Like you're a murderer?" *God, please don't let him be in on this.* She hoped with all that was inside her he was trying to save her, even if that meant pointing a gun at her. But she'd be stupid to believe him.

"Kirk is the one who is going to kill you," he said.

"Why? What's this all about? Please tell me something."

Unwilling to allow this man to abduct her and take her who knew where, she reached for the door handle and opened the car door.

I have to jump now. Before it's too late.

* * *

Riding a motorcycle two cars behind, Kirk watched the two-door sedan's passenger door fly open. Cora! What was going on? Was she trying to escape Lance?

He'd obviously threatened her or else she wouldn't have gotten into the car. He could be taking her somewhere to kill her, then dispose of her.

Seeing Lance alive had stunned him. The man had survived the explosion.

He could have been the one to set the bomb. He could have killed Captain Menken. Dressed like the captain to fool anyone who had seen him approach the island, and in Kirk's case, seen him leaving the *Sea Dragon*, not that it mattered because Kirk was supposed to have died in the blast.

Lance had faked his own death, as it were.

Kirk saw it clearly now. That traitor wanted to be thought dead, but he'd had to come back from the grave because Cora had escaped Judd.

Anger roiled through him as he throttled up the bike and passed one of the cars but kept one vehicle between himself and the sedan. He would make Lance pay if he hurt Cora…he would make them *all* pay.

If Cora could just stay alive long enough for him to safely get her away from Lance, then she had a fighting chance. But if she acted rashly and tried to jump out, she could get herself killed. The sedan was only doing fifty miles per hour, for which he was glad because he needed to catch up and keep up. This old motorcycle needed a tune-up and was barely worth the two hundred bucks he'd paid for it. Still, he was much too far away to help Cora.

The vehicle swerved and the door shut. Either she'd

pulled it shut or the force of the wind pushed it closed as the car accelerated.

God, please keep her safe. And if You're willing, please don't let me fail her again.

He'd let her down once already, when he'd assured her she would be safe with Judd. He couldn't have been more wrong. Time to make up for that mistake. He would follow, but not too close. Since he wore a helmet, he wouldn't be easily recognized, but he didn't want to risk giving himself away.

The last thing he wanted to do was get into a position where Lance would use Cora against him.

Kirk had spotted the *Clara Steele* in the marina parked in the wrong slip. He'd gone to look for Cora and had found Judd tied up, along with a sticky note on the door from Cora in her swirly handwriting.

Don't trust him, Kirk. He is one of the bad guys. He tried to drug me with tea.

By then, he'd already known that Judd had betrayed them. He'd double crossed them. He hadn't been sure how Cora could have gotten the best of a man like Judd, but he left the man tied up. She knew her knots, and though a sailor, Judd wouldn't get out of those knots without help and maybe even a good knife. That Judd had betrayed him like this was a near lethal stab to his gut. It sickened him. But he didn't have time to worry why Judd had done it, or about what to do with the man he once considered a close friend, so he left him and went in search of Cora before a killer could find her.

Her note hadn't told him where she would be. She couldn't afford to. But anyone who knew the island—that would include the *Sea Dragon* crew members—would be able to figure that Cora's best chance was to get off the island and the only way off, without a boat, was the ferry.

Lance had figured that out…and Kirk had been right behind him. He almost hadn't made it in time to witness what transpired, but thankfully he had. And when he'd seen Cora and Lance at a table inside the internet café, for a brief moment, Kirk had entertained the idea that she was complicit in this whole thing. But he'd just as quickly banished the thought.

In his heart, he knew Cora. He knew that she couldn't be involved in murder and destruction. Still, her willingness to go with Lance had tripped him up at first, but then, in the end, Kirk had seen Lance forcing her into the car.

Kirk had been too far away to make it in time. Calling out her name could have gotten her killed. His approach had to be stealthy. He'd heard mention of Lance trying to kill her and knew those were not idle threats. Trip had been involved and Lance had killed him.

Had he also killed Drake?

Despite his questions, he knew that Cora was in lethal danger. Facing off with Lance couldn't happen soon enough.

Bicycle riders crowded the streets and the sedan had to slow down and weave its way through the throng, as did Kirk. As soon as the riders thinned out, Kirk followed the speeding sedan straight out of town and into the mountainous region of the island.

Now he was the only vehicle behind the sedan. It would be more difficult for Kirk to remain anonymous, but all that mattered was the fact that he couldn't lose sight of Cora.

He didn't get how Judd was connected or why he'd

assisted them to begin with and kept them safe when someone tried to kill them. Kirk was definitely missing something. Had Judd's assistance simply been a ruse because he didn't want to get his hands dirty with murder involving his old navy buddy?

Oh, Judd. Why did you get involved with this?

Kirk found he had to distance himself even more from Lance and Cora to avoid being detected. Where was the guy taking her? Who would be waiting for them? The deep green rain forest lining the curvy roads thickened, and the road twisted up until switchbacks led them up the tallest mountain on Farrow Island.

He would have enjoyed this ride under any other circumstances. But not today. Adding to that, the bike began to sputter.

Come on, baby... Come on...

As if he could keep the bike moving with his sheer will.

When Lance turned down a private drive that disappeared through the trees, Kirk ditched the motorcycle. He would have to hike in on foot now. He stayed in the cover of the thick foliage and followed the drive and the sound of the sedan.

Who did the property belong to?

Kirk made his way through the dense vegetation, swatting away mosquitoes, wishing he had full military gear so he could steal Cora away in a quick and easy operation. The sedan was already parked in front of a spacious, luxurious log home that had to have cost ten years of his salary. Kirk tugged out binoculars he'd snagged from Judd's boat and remained at a distance to take in the property.

If Lance had wanted her dead, she would be.

Kirk charging in now would only get her killed. But his insides twisted into knots at the thought of Lance hurting her. Leaving her in there would mean just that. Lance obviously wanted information from her.

Through the binoculars, he spotted Cora. She stared out through a massive panoramic window on the south side of the home and rubbed her arms as if chilled. But he knew her—he knew that posturing. She was scared.

He zoomed in on her face—her beautiful face.

Cora, I'm so sorry I trusted the wrong person with your safety.

From now on, he alone would keep her safe. But first he had to get her out of this so he *could* keep her safe. Steal her away quietly, if he could, then call Jackson. He'd gone as far as he could with this case.

Kirk had heard enough to know these men were involved in murder and the destruction of the *Sea Dragon*. He'd discovered information about a code—which he suspected could be a dead drop. His part was done. He couldn't get to the bottom of Drake's death when Cora was in the thick of it.

Jackson would just have to be disappointed in Kirk. And…if Cora was safe, alive and well, then Kirk was okay with that. In fact, more than okay. It was all he wanted.

Kirk formulated a plan for getting into the home and finding Cora before Lance could hurt her. If the timing was off, Lance could use Cora against Kirk.

The jerk himself came up behind Cora as he approached the panoramic window. Giant shades rolled down and covered the window, blocking Kirk's view of what would happen next.

EIGHT

Goose bumps erupted on Cora's arms as the mechanical shades continued their descent, closing off the panoramic view and effectively shutting her off from the rest of the world. Her pulse pounded in her ears, drowning out all other sounds. She was a captive in this house with Lance. He stood behind her.

Right behind her.

Much too close.

No matter how much she rubbed her arms, she couldn't shake the chill, shake her fear.

What was he going to do with her now?

Before the shades had covered the window, she'd looked out, unable to enjoy the gorgeous view. But she'd stared into the woods and tried to hang on to the hope that Kirk would find her and save her life again, like he'd done so many times today. It seemed so surreal.

How long had it been since she'd first gone diving early this morning? More than twelve hours. How could so much have happened in such a short time?

Dusk had been closing in on the woods, much like danger was closing in around her. Darkness would descend much too soon.

God, help me out of this. Help me find a way to escape.

There was simply no way it was humanly possible for Kirk to find her, much less get her out of this mess. She would have to save herself. She wished she could have jumped from the car. Maybe she would have if Lance hadn't sped up instead of slowing down, but as the road rushed beneath her, she'd known she would die if she jumped.

There had been no other chance to escape. Now here she was in the lion's den.

Except Lance wanted her to believe he was protecting her.

Cora wasn't sure what Lance expected of her. What he wanted from her. She moved away from him to stand in the center of the massive great room and took in the rustic decorations, including a few animal heads. Gross.

She was almost surprised he allowed her to step away from him. Allowed her the freedom. But it had to do with this facade that he was protecting her by bringing her here. She'd go along with Lance's insistence that he was taking care of her, and that would give her time to make a plan to flee.

Why did people keep pretending they wanted to protect her? It wasn't like she was a damsel in distress, yet, on the other hand, maybe anyone would need help surviving under the circumstances.

But since no one else was here she had to rely on her own devices to get out of this, *if* she could come up with something. And she suspected that her chances of escape diminished the longer she remained with this creep. Others affiliated with Lance and his plans would likely show up soon. But right now, she *was* alone with him and she had no choice but to try to take him out like she'd taken Judd out.

Did Lance know what she'd done to Judd? Was he the man on the other end of the phone line to whom Judd had intended to take her?

Lance approached her again, and Cora tried to hide her fear by allowing her irritation to rise. He cupped her cheeks. She held back a shudder and blinked back tears before they could surge. Lance. On the *Sea Dragon*, he'd been good to her. Had shown interest in her, but she hadn't been ready or able. He'd acted like he might wait until she was ready to engage with him romantically. But then Kirk had joined the crew, and admittedly, he'd sucked up all Cora's attention.

"Cora, listen," Lance said softly. "I'm sorry I had to force you here. Please don't be mad at me. But like I already told you—it's for your own protection. You're safe here now with me. Are we good?" His dark blue eyes looked through her. Searching. He wanted to know the truth from her.

She couldn't speak the truth. She couldn't give him what he wanted to hear so she merely nodded. A smile lifted the corners of his lips, and he kind of looked like he wanted more than to keep her safe. He'd gotten her away from Kirk, and now he wanted her attention all to himself, and not in a way that she wanted to give.

She had to redirect him. She took a step back and he released her. She could breathe now. "What is this place?"

"It belongs to a friend. You have the run of the place, Cora. Think of it as a kind of safe house. I'm glad I got to you in time. Kirk would have killed you. You believe me now, don't you?"

No. Then she realized something. He could have been the diver who attacked them after the *Sea Dragon* went down. That would make sense.

Courage rose to the surface. She could lie to him to stay alive. "Working on the research vessel, I've known you for a long time, Lance. Of course I believe you." The weird thing? Cora wasn't entirely sure she knew why she couldn't trust what he told her, but call it a sixth sense. For another thing, he'd forced her with a gun. Kirk would never have done that. In fact, he wouldn't have forced her to stay on the boat with Judd and had let her make her own choice.

Lance studied her again, as though trying to read her.

She hoped she could be convincing. "I still don't understand why Kirk would want to harm me. Or what he's after. What is this all about? I have a million questions." *How are you still alive?*

She wouldn't think about the implications of his survival—who he'd killed. That he could have been the one to rig the explosions.

Still, she might as well get answers if Lance could give them.

"All in good time," he said. "I'm still trying to figure it out. As I've said, I had gone to the authorities, but after being nearly killed there, I'm not sure they can protect us until it's resolved. So here we are."

Had he really gone to the police? Hmm.

He eased her close and wrapped his arms around her in a warm hug. Her arms stiff, she forced herself to return the gesture while she squeezed her eyes shut. Her knees gave out, but Lance caught her up.

"Are you okay?"

"No, I'm… I'm exhausted. After everything that's happened."

Lance ran his fingers through her hair, becoming entirely too familiar with her. By the look in his eyes, he might actually care for her, but she wouldn't believe it. Someone had tried to kill her, and right now Lance was her number-one suspect. The question was—why was he letting her live now?

"I'm so glad you survived the explosion," he said. "And I'm so sorry this happened to you."

His nearness, his words, unnerved her. She stepped away. "I…I need to rest. Could I lie down for a bit?"

When his cell rang and interrupted them, irritation flashed in his eyes. "Sure. My room is the first one on the right."

He gestured to the hallway.

What? He expected her to sleep in *his* room? Bile rose in her throat.

She slowly made her way to the hallway, then crept along until she found the first door to the right. Hesitating, she looked behind her. Maybe while he was on the phone she could make a break for it.

She *had* to escape. It was now or never. But if she ran down this hallway, would she find a way out?

She had a feeling Lance intended to use her in ways she didn't want to fathom. She had to hurry. Moisture spread on her palms. She never would have believed him capable of any of this. She took a step away from his room then felt his eyes on her back. Too late. She couldn't get away with it. Not yet.

Aware that he watched her, she entered the first room on the right. His room. And shut the door. After a few seconds passed, she cracked it open so she could potentially hear what he said.

He spoke in low tones and sounded worried. Maybe even scared.

Interesting.

"Higgins will come for her here where I'll be waiting to face off with him. I'll show that agent who thought he could hide his true identity that he never should have interfered."

Then he lowered his voice even more, and she could hear no more. Quietly, Cora closed the door completely. She pressed her back against it while her heart hammered.

They would kill Kirk. Lance had called him an agent. He was working undercover? She didn't know him at all. Not like she thought she did.

He'd lied to her—in a manner of speaking.

She couldn't think about the hurt, the deception now. His life was in even more danger than it already had been if he actually found her and tried to save her, because Lance was expecting him. That must be the whole reason behind keeping her alive—to draw Kirk here.

She'd thought it had been for what she knew. What a joke. She didn't know anything. At least nothing they didn't already know. Whoever *they* were. Who else worked with Lance and Judd? Coburn? Captain Menken? Others on the crew?

She sucked in a breath to clear her head. She had to focus on the task. Get out of here. Cora rushed around the bed to the window. Could she climb out?

Her escape couldn't be this easy unless Lance really did trust her. Believed she trusted him. For crying out loud, he thought she wanted to sleep with him! No way. Not. Ever.

A desk sat under the window. She tried the drawers. Locked. Maybe she should have stayed behind to hear what else he would say, but what did it matter if she couldn't deliver the information?

Lance's voice grew louder, which meant he was coming to check on her. She had nothing with which to hit him in the head like she'd done to Judd. Cora dove for the king-size bed and curled in a fetal position. Closed her eyes. She forced her breathing to calm.

The door quietly opened.

Oh, no. Please, let him think I'm asleep. Let him believe I need the rest.

His footfalls were soft as he crept around the bed to stand over her. She was absolutely certain she was going to panic. Then she felt his lips against hers. A quick, gentle kiss. She kept her eyes closed and merely rolled over as if he'd disturbed her but not enough to wake her. That would be more natural, wouldn't it?

He left the room and closed the door.

It had worked! She could hardly believe it had worked. He thought she cared for him and would wait in this bed for him.

The fool!

She quietly left the bed, locked the door and went back to the window. But wait. A desk in this room could reveal secrets. The drawers were locked. All of them. She didn't have time to pick them.

But taking a closer look at the desk she found a piece of letterhead with the name Drake Jackson.

This was *his* home? The place he'd stayed when he

wasn't on the *Sea Dragon*? He'd gone missing. Was presumed dead. Was he alive or was he dead?

On the other side of the door pots and pans clanked. Lance cooking her a romantic dinner? Ugh!

She really needed to get into these drawers, after all. Seemed strange that he would let her stay in a room that held any sensitive information. Still…

Cora found a paper clip and went to work on the file drawers. It only took a moment—these desk locks were ridiculously easy to open. The file with that same triangular symbol that she'd seen on Judd's laptop was right there on top.

She skimmed the contents. Money transfers. Drug transfers. USB drives. Dates and locations. She recognized those locations all too well—shipwrecks that had supposedly been spotted. More often than not, those "finds" had turned out to be nothing. Had those tips been faked so they could exchange drugs and money for large volumes of information on a USB drive containing data? All for…data? Like they were using the so-called sneakernet, when someone didn't want their IP address associated with the transfer of information or the information was too massive to transfer quickly.

What *kind* of data?

Some of this was in a foreign language. She couldn't read it. But some of it she could understand. Navy propulsion and command-and-control technology.

Her gut clenched. Military secrets? No!

A heavy sigh resounded from behind her. Cora's heart stopped.

"Cora, Cora…" Deep disappointment threaded Lance's voice. "You know, I really thought you and I had a thing going. I had hoped my gut was wrong about you. But I see you failed my test."

Oh. Now she saw what she hadn't seen before. Of course. Of course! He'd put her in this room to see if she would take the bait.

Stupid, stupid girl. Maybe she could convince him she was still on his side. Fake it somehow. The way her hands were shaking—no. It was too late.

She dropped the file back into the drawer and shut it. He'd quietly unlocked the door and caught her red-handed. There was no hiding that truth now. Unsure where she found the courage, she slowly turned and faced Lance.

Now he would kill her.

It's now or never.

Aiming at Lance's torso, Kirk fired multiple rounds from his weapon. The window shattered.

The next few seconds unfolded in slow motion.

Cora's scream scorched the air as she ducked behind a filing cabinet.

Lance yanked a hidden gun out and fired three shots out of the now-broken window. Directly at Kirk. He ducked out of the way in the nick of time. Then he kept shooting as he tried to climb through the window, but the remaining glass shards clawed at him, digging into his skin like knives and slowed his progress so much they prevented him from climbing through the window. No way could he climb in quickly enough to avoid taking a bullet. Instead, he held his weapon, aimed and ready, but then Lance pointed his gun at Cora. *God, no, please no...*

The man would go to great lengths to use her against

Kirk, and he had no doubt Lance would kill her, too. That he would pull that trigger.

"Drop your weapon, Agent Higgins, or I'll shoot her."

Not if I shoot you first. Kirk fired his weapon at Lance, who twisted to return fire at Kirk.

Kirk had missed his chance at a kill shot, but he'd wounded Lance.

Angry, the man cried out and scrambled through the door. At least Kirk had stolen Lance's chance to shoot Cora.

She rushed to the door and locked it. That would buy them seconds. She bounded over to the window as he broke away the shards.

"Cora, are you all right?" He wanted to pull her through and against him. Needed to feel her safe in his arms.

"Yes. What about you? I was so worried about you. How did you find me?"

"We can talk about that later. We need to get you out of here. Now let me pull you through. Be careful of the glass."

"No."

"Cora, what are you doing? We have to get out of here."

"Everything we need is in these files. I'm not leaving without the information."

"Lance isn't dead. He could come back at any moment. We could miss our chance to leave without someone getting hurt." What was he saying? If she was right and the file contained the information he needed, this could be the mother lode.

Except all he could think about was getting her out of here.

"But don't you see? It won't end until we find out what is going on."

Right. She was right. He crawled through the window into the room.

"Okay, what did you find?" He moved to stand next to her against the desk.

She pulled a drawer open. "He set this up as a test to see if I would snoop, which I did, of course."

Kirk wanted to question her about everything that had transpired but he let it drop for now.

"Here." She tugged out the file she'd found.

"If he planted this, how do you know any of it's true?"

"See for yourself." She handed it over.

They should have taken the file and gotten out of there, but curiosity got the best of him and he opened it up.

She peered over his shoulder and pointed. "The file name. It's a symbol, see that?"

"Trigon." It had been next to the code name he'd found.

"That's what Lance called the ROV. He named it after an evil character in a comic book."

Kirk nodded. Now it was beginning to make sense. "And also the name of an old double-agent spy during the Cold War who worked via dead drops."

"That's what I saw. A gray box with that symbol."

Her words gave him pause. He pulled his gaze up to her. "You saw it? When?"

"I remembered everything about the dive, Kirk. Coburn and Trip had argued about something. I followed them down. They didn't know it. I shouldn't have been so irresponsible. But something was going on. I followed them…"

Seeing the tears pooling in her eyes, Kirk set the file aside. He gripped her arms. "Tell me everything you remember."

"I saw the box, the symbol and the surprise in their eyes when they spotted me. Then someone behind me cut my regulator hose." She choked out the next words. "The man held me from behind. Wouldn't let me escape, but I used my knife to free myself and swam away."

"You made it on your own. I found you washed up on a sandbar. I performed CPR. I…" Now it was his turn to choke. He couldn't finish the words. He'd thought she was dead. He hadn't known if he could actually revive her. "The diver who cut your hose. You didn't see his face, then?"

"No."

"We'll take the file and read it later. We need to get out of here. I'll call my contact."

"Wait. Your contact?" Her eyes widened. "I overheard Lance calling you an agent."

Okay. Well, it was time to tell her everything, but not here. Not now. "I'll explain later. Since Lance is somewhere in the house, we'll just climb out the window and escape through the woods."

"Wait. How do you know he's not waiting for us out there?"

"I shot him. He's wounded. It'll take him time to see to that if he wants to live, so we have to hurry. I have a motorcycle hidden away that we can take. We'll get on the next ferry out of here to Seattle where I can hand the file over. I'm…done." Was he really? Would the file be enough to prevent him from disappointing Jackson regarding Drake? Or himself, if the file failed to give them the answers they needed about who'd killed his friend? He handed the file back to her. "Hold on to this."

Through the broken window they could make their escape. Darkness stared back at them from the thick forest. Even moonlight wouldn't penetrate. Leaves rustled and a twig snapped.

Someone was out there.

NINE

Someone was watching them!

Bullets sprayed the room.

Kirk snatched her away from the window and against the wall. His strong arms embraced her as he caught his breath. She was grateful the bullets hadn't come through the walls.

"That was too close. Are you okay?"

"Yes. I think so." Pulse racing, she pressed her cheek against his broad chest and listened to his heart beating strong and fast. He was scared? Worried for their safety? That wasn't good. Not good at all.

On the other hand, fight-or-flight adrenaline coursing through their veins could give them the boost needed to stay alive.

Releasing her, Kirk took her hand and, keeping flat against the wall, led her over to the door where he flipped off the lights sending them into complete darkness.

"What are you doing?" She kept her voice low.

"What do you think? If whoever is out there can't see us, they can't shoot us."

Made sense. "But now what?"

"Shh," he whispered. "Obviously, we have to go through the house."

"Lance is still inside, isn't he? He could try to kill us again."

Kirk didn't respond. Maybe he thought they had a better chance in the house with an injured man than in the woods against an unknown foe who also wanted to kill them. He positioned her behind him and quietly opened the door, his gun at the ready. He peered out into the hallway, looking both left and right, then took a step out of the room.

Okay...

They crept down the dimly lit corridor toward the great room. What if Lance was there? Cora wished she had explored the house. If she had, she would know where the back door was and they could escape that way. She might have discovered more ways to leave. Or found more incriminating evidence.

Kirk motioned for her to wait behind him as he peered around a corner to make sure it was clear. Not the first plan she would have chosen. She didn't see them waltzing out the front door so easily, and neither should he.

After all, he was a hotshot agent of some kind, wasn't he?

And that meant he must know a whole lot more about what was going on than he let on. That had been the whole reason for his joining the *Sea Dragon* crew, hadn't it?

The front door opened. Lance could be heard swearing at someone. In the woods? Over the phone?

Kirk suddenly pressed his back against the wall. He

ushered her quietly down the dark hall that led to the back of the house.

Footfalls resounded behind them.

"Hurry!" Kirk pushed her faster.

"Where are we going?"

"You!" A voice blasted from behind.

Gunfire rang out. A bullet whizzed by her head, right past her ear. Goose bumps crawled over her at the close call. Kirk tried to open a door but it was locked.

Another one.

A bullet slammed into the wall.

He shoved his foot at the door and kicked it open. Thrusting her inside, he practically tossed her to the floor.

"Stay here!" He shut the door behind him.

Cora wanted to open it. To be with him and help him. To follow him. But she could get in the way and endanger his life. Endanger both their lives.

Leaving the lights off, she crossed her arms and waited with her back against the wall far from the window. Tension corded her neck.

More gunfire exploded on the other side of the door.

Rubbing her arms, she paced the small dark space. Cora couldn't stand it. She had to do something to help. But what? Maybe she could find a weapon in a drawer. More files. More answers. Something. Light shone from beneath the door, allowing her to see a few things. A side table. She opened the drawers and rustled through for a weapon.

Nothing!

Oh, wait. Something. A small book. She thumbed through it, the words on the pages barely visible in the dark room. Someone's handwriting. A diary? Maybe it was important. She tucked it away in her pocket, though it wouldn't save her.

After slamming the drawers, she let her gaze travel to the lamp on the table.

The wall shuddered. Grunts and groans met her ears. The two men were fighting now, instead of shooting? Someone growled in pain. Oh, no!

Had it been Kirk?

The brass lamp. A lamp had worked for her before against a large beast of a man.

She reached for her weapon of choice and quietly opened the door.

A man stood with his back to her and his gun pointed at Kirk. Her heart dropped to her gut. Kirk was on the floor, leaning against the wall, a horrific, dazed expression on his face. His eyes grew wide when he saw her.

The man shifted around to look, his grimacing face scruffy and shadowed. His eyes narrowed but he couldn't react fast enough. Without hesitation, Cora swung the brass lamp full force against his temple. She squeezed her eyes shut as the lamp connected with flesh and bone. She couldn't look at the violent act from her own hand. She didn't want to see the blood.

Oh, Lord, please don't let him be dead. Just...out of commission for a while. Gasping for breath, she opened her eyes as he stumbled backward and fell face-first on the hardwood floor.

Would she need to hit him again? She hoped not. She moved closer to the assailant until she stood over him, ready to swing. Recognition hit her.

"Coburn?"

She dropped the lamp to the floor.

Next to her, Kirk bent over him. She released a breath as he grabbed the gun Coburn had dropped.

"Is he…is he dead?"

Kirk looked for a pulse and found one. "He'll survive."

He slowly stood tall, his face wet with exertion. Bloodied with the fight.

Her adrenaline running through her veins hard and fast, and her emotions out there, too, she suddenly wanted to kiss him, and kiss him hard.

A lump grew in her throat. This wasn't the time for crazy, but she couldn't pull her gaze away from his deep blue eyes, which seemed to reveal the same need.

"You're hurt." She pressed a finger against the purpling knot on his head.

The lights suddenly went out.

Lance! Or was there someone else involved? Coburn was on the floor. Trip was dead. Judd—had he escaped?

Though she couldn't see a thing, Kirk grabbed both her hands with just one of his and squeezed.

"Don't worry about me." He spoke in a low tone. "It could have been worse. Come on. We're getting out. Lance is back there. Coburn showed up. Who knows who else." He tugged her behind him, feeling his way along the completely dark hallway. Finding a door, he opened it, pulling her through.

"Wait," she said. "You can't see where you're going. You could fall down a staircase or… I don't know."

He switched on a flashlight. They were in a game room with a pool table.

Cora almost laughed.

"Satisfied?"

"Yes."

"Good, because now I'm turning it off." The room went dark again.

"Why did you do that?"

"We don't want to be the only light shining for miles around, do we?"

"I see your point. So, we're taking the window now, since the front door is out, right?"

"Yep. In spite of the fact someone is out there. We can hope they're in the house now. It could have been Coburn out there shooting at us to begin with. Or Scott or Chuck—they're in this, too."

She gasped. "No. I can't believe it. They've always been so nice."

"The window is our only escape at the moment, Cora. Let's hurry. Then we'll have to get as far away from this Trigon business as possible."

Kirk quietly unlocked and opened the window, punched out the screen, then slid out into the darkness and down what appeared to be a hefty drop—this side of the house was built up on a hill. The moon broke through the canopy, giving her a glimpse of him as he reached up like he would catch her.

Her heart tumbled just a little at the sight. If only...

On the other hand, was he kidding? She wasn't about to attempt to jump into his arms in the dark. "I can make it."

Cora climbed through the window, then gripped the edge as she hung from it, reducing the distance. She prepared to drop the rest of the way but Kirk caught her by the waist and lowered her.

Without a word or a whisper, he took her by the hand.

She hoped he could see where they were going because she couldn't, and she would trip and fall a thousand times without something to light the way. And she did just that.

Her foot caught on a fallen branch and she fell forward, letting out a yelp. Give her a murky, dark dive in the ocean any day of the week.

Kirk hefted her into his strong arms. She didn't need his help but the guy was relentless in his effort to protect her now. He would barely let her get a foot away from him.

"What are you doing? Put me down."

"Keep quiet, please," he whispered. His breath fanned her cheeks. He was entirely too close.

"How can you see in this?"

"I'm wearing night-vision goggles."

"Why didn't I know that? Oh, that's right. There's a lot I don't know about you. You're a special agent. Lance said so."

"First, I pulled these off Coburn when we were fighting. It's how he made his way around out here. And second, it sounds like you think that Lance is someone you should believe."

"Well? Was he lying?"

She gripped him as he trampled through the forest, taking entirely too long to reply.

"No."

Cora waited for further explanation but got none. Would she ever? She didn't press him at the moment because they were making their escape. Finally, he stopped and lowered her next to a large boulder at the base of a ridge. The moon broke through and she could see him well enough. He tugged off the goggles. Brandished his weapon.

Bent over his knees and caught his breath. "It's gone."

"What are you talking about?"

"I left an old motorcycle here. It's how I followed you. I bought it off someone in town." He shot her a disbelieving look. "I saw that crazy move you made to get away from Lance, by the way—the one where you opened the door and planned to jump out of a moving vehicle."

"I thought I could make it but I changed my mind."

"Glad you did. As for the missing transportation, we could have made our mad escape on it. But someone took off with it. It's not here where I left it."

"What kind of secret agent *are* you? Or are you a double agent, like the Trigon character you mentioned?" And Cora knew too much. *Oh, Lord, please, don't let him be a bad guy, after all. I've spent the last several hours convincing myself he was the good guy.*

He huffed a laugh and settled on the ground against the rock to rest. "Nothing so intriguing." He hesitated, as if reluctant to say more, then offered, "Thank you."

"For what?" Cora decided to join him and dropped to the ground next to him. The night was cool but they'd been making their way through the woods. She wasn't chilled yet.

"For saving my life. You're very good with a lamp, by the way. Almost as good as you are with a speargun."

"I don't know. I think I might be better with the lamp."

He chuckled. She loved hearing the sound. It was a welcome reprieve from everything. Except… "So, tell me who you are. What kind of agent are you, Kirk?"

"I'm NCIS."

"NC… Naval Criminal Investigative Service."

"That's right."

"So you weren't looking for a job on the *Sea Dragon*, after all. You wanted to be part of the crew to investigate this…this whatever it is. Trigon."

"I didn't know about Trigon. I was trying to find out what happened to another crew member."

She tried to control her breathing and the way her heart hammered inside. She hated lies. Hated that she always seemed to trust the liars. Fury crashed over her. All those times he'd asked her to trust him…

"All this time, and you've been lying about your identity."

"Cora…"

"It's okay. It makes perfect sense. It rings true that you lied."

His heart seized up, then stumbled around. She'd meant like Stephan. A man who had betrayed her in the worst way. Stunned at how much her accusation, her comparison hurt, he blinked away the burn in his eyes.

What could he say to that?

He didn't blame her for making that connection. But didn't she get it? "This isn't the same. I was—I *am*—working undercover. It's my job to get answers. Although maybe not anymore, since I'm pretty sure that my cover is blown." He scraped a hand through his hair.

He was running out of time to get the information back to Jackson. Soon he'd have to report in to Matt, his NCIS superior, and he still didn't know whom he could trust in all this.

"I get it," she said, but nothing more. She didn't expound after making her proclamation.

Insects chirped. A couple of bats swooped and dove,

searching for dinner. While the night sounds could relax him, he would prefer hearing Cora telling him that she understood.

That she…forgave him.

Through all of his efforts to keep her safe, he'd realized that, without a doubt, years ago he should have tried harder. He should have stood his ground when Stephan had made moves on Cora. Of course, she might have preferred his brother to begin with, but he could still remember that hurt look in her eyes when Stephan asked her out. She had looked to Kirk for some sort of confirmation that she belonged to him or was with him or even that he was interested in her. Fighting for her, maybe. At the time, he'd thought he was letting her choose—he had wanted her to choose him over Stephan. Stupid, stupid mistake. He hadn't been surprised when she had chosen his more charming brother. It had happened before, after all. If only he could do it over again, he would have shown Cora exactly how he felt about her.

But it was too late. They couldn't go back. More than anything he wanted her to understand this one thing. "Cora. There's something you need to know, in case you don't already."

"What's that?" Her voice sounded soft, distant.

"I'm not my brother." What was he doing? Dragging all this up. They needed to get moving soon.

She didn't speak for a while, then, finally, said, "Did I ever tell you about the reason I became a shipwreck archaeologist?"

"No." In fact, they never got that far. Stephan probably didn't know, either. Knowing his brother like he did, Kirk figured Stephan probably never even asked her. "Please tell me. I'd love to hear the story."

Love to hear everything about the woman he thought he could fall for and maybe even had, a little, before.

Folding her arms around her knees, she leaned forward. Her short hair spiked up, revealing her long neck. He resisted the urge to rub her back. They really should get moving, but if they were going to have to hike all the way to town, they needed to rest.

"My grandfather had a collection of those ships in a bottle."

He chuckled.

"Have you ever seen one?"

"Yes."

"He made them himself. Talk about fascinating to watch. He would tell me stories to go with the ships. Inspired my imagination. When we would go to the beach, I used to pretend that I would find a ship in a bottle washing up on the beach. Or a message in a bottle. I don't know. My young mind kind of mixed things up on that point."

"Oh, I don't know. I think anything washing up in a bottle would be fascinating."

"Then, as I grew older, other girls were interested in cheerleading or the boys they would date. But I just kept dreaming about ships, only not in bottles. The kind that had sunk. Shipwrecks. And it was not *just* about the shipwrecks, but the stories of the people who were on the ships. I longed to learn their stories and tell them. Like my grandfather. He had Alzheimer's and disappeared. Got lost. We...we never found him."

"I'm sorry, Cora."

She swiped at her eyes.

"In his memory, if I could tell the story of even one person who was lost—the story of what happened, then I would be happy."

"So you ended up becoming a marine archaeologist."

She chuckled. "I figured the shipwrecks and the people who went down with them have tales that need to be told. I was living my dream on that research vessel that went down, working with all those people every day. People I thought I could trust."

"I'm...so sorry. You know, there are probably many crew members who, like you, are completely innocent."

"I'm not done."

"Okay." Against his better judgment, he placed his hand against her back and rubbed it. The night air had grown chilly.

"I'm good at digging into things. Finding the truth. Maybe that's what's happened here. I opened that file and I found out about Drake. I believe that was his house...and that he was keeping a file on everything there. He was involved, somehow."

Kirk dropped his hand and sat up, leaning forward to look at her face in the shadows. "What did you say? You think that was *Drake's* house?"

"Yes. Why?"

"My investigation, the reason I joined the crew, was to find out what happened to Drake."

"And the files prove he was involved. But why was he killed?"

No. He couldn't believe that. Maybe he was too close to be investigating this, after all. Under any other circumstances he wouldn't have been trusted with this investigation, but Jackson wanted answers.

Kirk blew out a long breath.

"Drake was my best friend growing up." He thought about what Cora had shared with him about the reasons she became a shipwreck archaeologist. "I think that was the whole reason I ended up here, now, at this moment in time, with you."

"What?"

"As you know, my dad's an attorney. Higgins and Sons. I was supposed to join the family business."

"But you ended up in the navy. Why?"

"I'd always been fascinated with the ocean. Drake's dad took us fishing all the time. My father was too busy. But I couldn't get enough of the water. I would daydream about being out there all day. Eventually I realized I couldn't become a lawyer, but I had waited far too long to tell my family what I was thinking. They had already made plans for me, of course."

She pressed her palm against his arm. "So you feel like you let them down. You disappointed them by not becoming a lawyer."

"Right. Stephan was the good son. I was the black sheep in the family."

"I'm so sorry."

"It's water under the bridge, as they say. They have a son who did what they wanted. So, anyway, when Drake and I were kids, we'd hang out on the beach. And one day…we found a body on the shore. A boy just like us. Nobody ever found out what happened to him. So I think I always had a part of the lawyer mind-set in me—I wanted to get justice, even if it was delayed justice."

"So that's why you're working for the investigations division of the navy."

"Yes."

"Digging for the truth, just like me. We're kindred spirits, aren't we?"

He felt her smile, more than saw it. His heart warmed.

Cora…

More than anything he wanted to reach out and pull her to him. Kiss her. That feeling he'd had the first time he saw her—that he wanted her to be his—had never left. What was it about her, anyway? Maybe they were kindred spirits, like she said. But talking about his family and what a disappointment he'd always been to them—reminded him that he feared he would never be good enough. Feared he would disappoint Cora in the end.

But that's why he had to finish this. Find out what had happened to Drake. He couldn't let Commander Jackson down. That man had been more like a father to him than his own father. He'd taken him fishing and he'd given him the love of the ocean.

"Thanks for sharing that with me. I know you're not like your brother, Kirk. I know that you're not a liar. I'm sorry I said that. I just needed to hear you try to convince me, I guess. And you did."

Suddenly Cora leaned in and kissed him gently.

TEN

What am I doing?

She really didn't know, but she couldn't help herself. His story moved her to the core. Touched something deep inside that she thought she'd buried for good.

She thought to end the kiss. But his hand pressed gently against the base of her head, fingers weaving through her hair and urging her closer. Kirk's response... She hadn't expected it. Her breath hitched at the tenderness, the emotion pouring from him as he deepened the kiss while at the same time, holding back.

Crazy to think that only moments before she'd been furious he'd lied to her. Kept all this hidden from her. And, well, yeah, he was working undercover and she shouldn't hold it against him for doing his job, but it made her think how easily he could lie.

Like Stephan.

"Cora..." Kirk whispered against her lips.

Her heart danced at the way he said her name.

No. He was nothing like Stephan. This man was good, so good to the core. He cared about justice. She saw that now. Understood him better.

Or maybe it was more that she *wanted* to believe him. "Kirk... I..." She eased away.

He kept his hold on her, looking into her eyes, and ran his thumb down her cheek. Turmoil swirled with raw emotions she couldn't define. An unexplainable connection.

Then they were shuttered away. "We should get going. We don't want them to find us."

She nodded and started to climb to her feet, but hesitated. "Wait. Let's look at the file. I don't know what's going to happen next. Maybe this will be our only chance to find out the truth." She met his eyes. "Maybe Drake was gathering information to take all this to the police. Did you consider that?"

"No. I hadn't. Thanks for thinking of a reason my best friend growing up could be innocent. You're good for me, you know that?" He cupped her cheek, then let his hand drop. He sighed. *What was that about?*

"You have a flashlight, don't you?"

In reply he flicked it on. She opened the files and together they perused the information. Cora showed Kirk what she had found so far. "So, they were using the locations to make transfers like an old spy movie dead drop. Exchanging information for drugs they would then sell to another contact. Although looks like sometimes it was cash and not drugs."

Nausea rolled through her. "I can't believe it. I can't believe any of them would use a research vessel for drugs. I don't understand it. I loved my job and now look what they did." But didn't drug deals often end in murder and destruction?

Kirk held the flashlight in one hand and rubbed his chin in the other, his brow furrowed. "There are a lot of names here. But a lot of missing names, as well. Trip's name isn't here and yet I found information on his laptop. He was there when the diver attacked you and didn't offer up the truth in the face of Coburn's lie."

"Maybe...maybe he wanted to," she said. "Maybe, like me, he was trying to figure things out. He was going to expose them, tell the truth about what happened to me, and that's when he was murdered."

"That's possible. Whatever the case, they were obviously discreet in bringing the drugs on board and then transferring them."

"I wonder how anyone on the *Sea Dragon* could miss what they were doing. But I missed it. That is, until I got curious about some of their activities. I suppose it helps the man in charge of security was in on it, too."

"What activities made you curious?" he asked.

"A late-night dive, for one. I'm talking the middle of the night when everyone else was asleep."

Kirk nodded, but said nothing. Had he known about those?

"I guess Trip got suspicious, too. That's why he took Coburn to dive that day. Maybe Trip was curious about things that didn't add up—I don't know what. I followed them both and that's when someone got to me."

"Maybe they tried to convince Trip to get in on it," Kirk said. "They would give him a cut. That has to be a lot of money and for some reason they believed Trip would take their offer. I found the code name on his laptop when I hacked it. At first I thought it was simply referencing the ROV."

"Again, he could have been gathering information and planned to turn them in so he was killed." She'd prefer to think of him as one of the good guys.

"You could be right. Whatever the case may be, I suspect there was someone else. Someone on the outside calling the shots. Someone who knew I was working undercover. That's the only reason I can think of to destroy the *Sea Dragon* and annihilate anyone who got in their way."

"Like you and me? And Trip."

He nodded solemnly.

"Who is it, then? Who's the person calling the shots, as you say?" she demanded. "It doesn't seem anyone knew who that person actually was. The information in this file doesn't mention his name."

"I could be wrong about it all. Maybe it was Coburn, Lance, Judd, Scott and Chuck. They got suspicious of me and figured it out. But there still has to be someone who passed along the USB drive with information."

"Right. And it was all done via digital communications, codes and dead drops." Her memory flashed. An image from their escape at Drake's home. "Oh, wait. I have something here." She tugged it out of her pocket. "I think it's a diary, of all things." She flipped it open and examined the first page. "Kirk...it's Drake's diary, which makes sense, of course. It was his house."

He wrapped his hands around hers and shut the book. "It could take all night to read this. We don't have all night. Let's find a way out of here, off this island and head to the authorities. Drake's father was the one to send me on this mission, Navy Commander Jackson."

"But we can't just turn this over to them. We have to read it first."

Kirk hesitated.

"Kirk? What are you thinking?"

He stood and pulled her to her feet. Stuck the diary in

his own pocket. Then gently gripped her arms. "Thank you for finding this. I should read the diary. Not you. I don't want you putting yourself in more danger. It could contain something…classified. Something that could get you killed even after we've resolved all of this."

"You want Drake to be innocent, don't you? But we already know that he's not."

"But like you mentioned, he could have been collecting evidence and was going to turn them all in, but someone got to him first. I wanted to find out who, but maybe I won't be the one to do that." He blew out a breath. "At the very least, I want to make sure you're somewhere safe, as in a safe house if that's what it takes, and this information gets to the right people before it's too late."

"How can you even know who they are?"

He scraped his hands through his hair. "One thing at a time, Cora. We've already been here too long."

He grabbed her hand and led her through the temperate rain forest. She hadn't realized that even a small island could take forever to hike. Finally, below them, Farrow Village came into view. It was still miles away. Cora wanted to collapse with exhaustion.

"Here, let me carry you."

She shoved him away. "No, don't even think about it." Though she really wanted to rest in his arms. Not only would that give her feet a break, she…well, she could be close to Kirk.

Maybe if they got through this alive and the dust settled, she and Kirk would get a second chance, but that would require her getting over her feelings of rejection, some of which Kirk had contributed to. Still, she wouldn't forget that kiss anytime soon, and the way

Kirk protected her now could almost make her forget the past and let go of her insecurities.

They continued hiking for another hour and made it through the village until they stood at the ferry terminal.

He pulled her into the shadows, so near to him she could smell his musky, masculine scent.

"You told me you'd bought a ticket," he said.

"Yes."

"Well, let's see if we can change it or get a new one and get off this island."

Relief swelled inside. She felt dirty and sticky and sweaty. A hot shower came to mind. "I can't think of anything I'd rather do."

Than leave this place, with Kirk, no less.

He smiled down at her as they headed toward the ferry. She'd been so relieved when he'd been there to prevent Lance from killing her. Relieved that he was with her now, but it was so much more than that. Her heart skipped a few beats. He'd come for her. It was so heroic. He was a protector, and not just any hero, not just any protector. *The* protector she'd imagined him to be. Maybe always wanted Kirk to be.

And, it suddenly occurred to her, all those years ago she had been the one to make a mistake the day she'd accepted Stephan's invitation for a dinner date—and had gone out with him even after witnessing the hurt in Kirk's eyes. She'd thought if he really wanted to be with her, he would have stood in his brother's way. She'd been disappointed when he hadn't. She'd been shocked and hurt, and in rebounding, she'd grown involved with Stephan—someone who had claimed to want her. Except, deep inside, she had never truly returned Stephan's supposed interest.

Deep inside, it had always been Kirk she had truly wanted.

What a foolish person she'd been.

Young and inexperienced.

And now, here she was, still keeping her heart from loving. She didn't know if he could still even want her even though his kiss said that maybe he did.

On the ferry they took seats, or rather, she took a seat. Kirk stared down at her, the same sadness and regret pouring from his gaze.

"What's wrong?" Her pulse jumped.

"I can't go with you."

"What?" She stood.

He pushed her back down. "I have to stay on Farrow Island. I brought you here because you can be safe. I have to find them and finish this."

"But you said we'd go to the authorities together. Was it all a lie to get me here?"

"It was true when I said it. But I've had a couple of hours to think about how best to proceed. There's something I'm missing in all this. It could be deadly to us. To you. So I'm leaving you where you'll be safe. You're heading back to Seattle. Go stay with Jonna and Ian or Sadie and Gage in Coldwater Bay for a few days. They'll know how to protect you. Don't call anyone else. Don't talk to anyone. Stay low until this is over."

She grabbed him. She didn't want to let him go. "Please, Kirk. Come with me. You have the file that Drake kept *and* his diary. What more do you need?" She was scared for him. That he would end up getting killed.

She was scared that even if he lived she'd never see him again.

"Call it a gut instinct, but I believe I'm missing something. I'm so close now to solving this and if I give up now, I could lose my chance to find the truth forever. Please understand." He lifted her hand and kissed it.

She held back the tears. "I understand. You have to find out what happened to Drake on your own."

"It's more that I want you to be safe. You have almost lost your life too many times. Use the burner phone I got you and call your sister."

"But what about you. How will I know you're okay?"

"I'll call you when it's over. When it's safe." He walked away, leaving her sitting there.

Cora fought the disappointment that swelled. Everything he said made perfect sense. He was the agent, after all. This was his job. He would be better off if he didn't have to protect her or worry about her. She'd seen that play out too many times for comfort. This was for the best.

But the feeling dogged her. She couldn't help but think this was the last time she would see Kirk…

Alive.

Kirk plopped into the seat in a dark corner of an internet café near the ferry terminal.

He'd crushed his own heart, sending her off like that. He would have no reason to see her again. But it was much more important that she was far from here and safe. He hadn't wanted to send her away. He would have preferred keeping her with him or better yet, going with her—but he had to finish this. It was better this way.

He set his own burner phone on the small table and

spun it. A part of him wished she would call him just so he could hear her voice. Or he could call her—but what would be the point? He would, however, call her in a few hours to make sure she was with one of her sisters. Jonna ran a storm-watching lodge on the coast. She and her husband were former agents with the feds, different divisions, but now together in private security. The two of them would watch out for her. Or her sister Sadie and her husband Gage. He was CGIS. Cora would be safe with them.

Now to get down to business.

Kirk pulled out Drake's old diary and set it on the table. He needed to skim through it to see if there was any additional incriminating information about who was involved in these nefarious activities. And also hopefully uncover who was responsible for Drake's death. Although, on that front, he had his suspicions.

One thing he knew for sure, Jackson would be severely disappointed to learn that his son had had any part in this kind of operation. And that's why Kirk had to have facts before he went marching into the commander's office to deliver the news. If it affected Kirk this hard, he couldn't imagine how hard Jackson would take it. The man might prefer to leave Drake's death a mystery.

The leather peeling and crusty, the diary was something Drake had had since he was a kid. Kirk opened it and began skimming but soon found himself reading it word for word. He read stories of their adventures and harrowing escapes—just two boys getting into mischief, the innocent kind, and having fun.

He laughed. He even cried.

But he wanted, *needed* this moment, this chance to

get back into Drake's head. As often happens, he and his childhood friend had gone their separate ways, pursuing their careers. He hadn't talked to Drake much in years.

Kirk wanted to understand his friend's mindset, if that was possible, by reading his diary. It could hold all the answers he sought.

Some of the more recent entries, well, he did end up skipping them. They were entirely too personal and he didn't want to invade Drake's privacy even though he was gone.

Then Kirk came upon the part he was searching for even as the man's writing style became dark and distressed, which made sense.

I'm gathering evidence against all the players. This has gone on long enough. I'm going to turn them in. I'm going to stop this before it's too late. I can't be part of turning over military secrets.

Kirk swallowed hard. *Oh, Drake, you didn't...*

He kept reading and learned that Drake had offered them a chance to stop and they hadn't taken it. Hadn't he realized that would get him killed? Closing his eyes, Kirk imagined Drake suffering from a fate similar to what someone had tried to inflict on Cora. Someone behind her—the unknown diver. The same diver who had attacked them after they escaped the bombs?

He forced his attention back to the diary and read further.

Lance and Judd were *brothers*? An incredulous huff escaped him.

His cell vibrated on the table. Cora. The call came from the burner he'd given her. His heart leaped at first. He'd wanted to hear her voice, then panic took hold. He hoped she hadn't run into trouble.

"Cora," he answered.

"She isn't able to answer the phone," Lance said. "Oh, wait, she didn't call you. I did."

"What have you done with her?"

"She's alive, don't worry."

Kirk worked to keep his voice steady. "Please don't hurt her."

"What will you do for us?"

"Anything."

Lance knew that, and that's why she'd been taken. Kirk had been such a fool. An idiot.

"Just tell me where to meet you."

"I don't trust you to meet us anywhere. Judd is waiting for you outside where you can hand over the cell phone. Go with him or I'll have to hurt her. Again." The man laughed.

Kirk ground his molars. "Why you—"

"I look forward to the chance to face off with you again, Special Agent Higgins, but I assure you that you'll definitely be on the losing end this time. I'm just sorry that Cora chose you over me."

"If you lay another hand on her—"

"You'll what? You have nothing with which to bargain. Now, do exactly as I say. Remain on the phone with me and walk outside to Judd. Do anything and I promise you'll hear her scream over the phone."

His throat constricted. Cora. Oh, Cora. He never should have left her. *God, please keep her safe!*

Kirk slowly rose from the table. He couldn't take the files and diary with him—the only real evidence he had. He searched the café. Near the table, a column to support the roof was awkwardly placed. Behind the column, he spotted a crack in the paneling near the floor. Perfect. He tucked the file and the diary in the crack, hoping he could retrieve it later. But at least no one would find the evidence here. Someone would have to know where to look to find it.

Taking a deep breath, he squared his shoulders, then strode through the door and spotted Judd.

"You still with me?" Lance asked over the phone.

"I see Judd. I'm walking toward him now."

"Good. Now, to make sure you don't try anything, here is a down payment on my promise."

Cora screamed.

ELEVEN

Oh, God, help me!

Cora hadn't wanted to give this man the satisfaction of making her scream. With a fistful of hair, he'd driven her to her knees. Even though she kept her hair short, he'd been able to grab enough to hurt her. Pain erupted from her scalp.

She sucked in a breath and bit her lip to hold back more groans.

Still, she had to warn Kirk. "Don't do it, Kirk! Don't—"

Lance smacked her, knocking her to the ground. Her face stung as she shook off the daze. At least she hadn't screamed again. While he stayed on the phone with Kirk, she crawled away from Lance and over to slump against the decking of the *Clara Steele*.

Coburn had a nasty bruise on his temple where Cora had hit him with the lamp last night—could it have been just last night when she'd hit him at Drake's house? So much had happened since then.

He scowled at her.

You deserved it!

He yanked her to her feet and took her belowdecks,

then shoved her into a stateroom. She turned around in time to spit in his face.

He slammed the door. She heard a lock click from the outside.

"How is it that you are reduced to nothing more than a drug smuggler? You're better than this, Coburn!" She banged on the door to no avail.

Why waste her time and energy? Cora huddled on the small twin bed in the corner. She would nurse her wounds for the moment and regroup. Figure a way out of this. She definitely wasn't climbing through the small porthole. There was no way to escape. She thought back to the events that led to her capture. Mere minutes after Kirk had left her on the ferry, Coburn had appeared at her side and forced her off the ferry with a gun.

She should have screamed. Refused. Something. But he claimed to have Kirk and that he would kill Kirk if she didn't go with him. It was hard to believe she'd worked alongside these guys and had gotten to know them. It was as if they were strangers. Maybe behind their crazed looks she could see the men she knew were still inside. But once they'd turned to the dark side, it seemed impossible to reason with them. However, she'd never really liked Coburn. Something had always seemed off about him.

To think she might have taken an interest in Lance— it made her skin crawl, especially when she considered that when this was all done her body would be thrown overboard.

There would be no one to find her and tell her story. It would be as if she had gone down with a ship—a shipwreck waiting to be discovered and the passengers' stories told, only she would be lost forever. Just like her grandfather, whom she'd loved so much.

Maybe that was a fitting end for her.

The door lock clicked again, as if someone was unlocking the door. Cora stirred at the sound and realized that she'd fallen asleep. Heart pounding, she stiffened as fear slithered through her. She'd been exhausted after the long day and night they'd had, so she wouldn't berate herself. Unfortunately, it hadn't all been a dream.

She sat up as the door swung open. So much for knocking. Lance leaned into the room. He'd been a looker but now he just looked strange to her. All that handsomeness wrapped around the biggest creep she'd ever met.

"Showtime."

He left the door open and disappeared.

"What do you mean?" she called after him.

Did he want her to follow? Cora wasn't a hundred percent sure she wanted to. If he'd left her then maybe she could make a run for it. But that was just it. Where would she go out in the middle of a large body of water? She would jump into the water and die of hypothermia eventually. They would get to her before she could swim away, even if she tried.

Maybe she would prefer to die trying to escape.

Cora eased from the bed and peeked out the door. She made her way down the hallway. What did they want from her? Had Kirk come, as they'd requested?

Of course he had. He was a hero first. He thought he'd been doing the right thing by sending her back to Seattle. She got that. And then things had gone horribly awry. She hadn't even had the chance to connect with

Jonna or Sadie before Coburn nabbed her. And now she could die out here and her sisters would never know what happened. She wasn't sure her brother Quinn would even care because she hadn't heard from him in much too long. She understood why—working DEA undercover could take a person to dark places around the world. She feared something had happened to him, like something was about to happen to her.

At the end of the hall she approached the steps that would take her up on deck. She lingered at the bottom. Voices resounded above. Heart hammering, she ascended the stairs, and once she rose above the deck to see what was going on, her gaze immediately connected with Kirk's.

From his position on his knees, hands bound behind his back, he looked at her, regret and sorrow in his eyes.

Her heart was going to break into a million pieces.

Seeing him like that—driven to the deck like she'd been—tormented her in ways she'd never experienced.

Oh, Kirk...

She hoped he read in her eyes that she didn't blame him. How much she cared for him—as if it mattered at the moment.

After all they had been through to escape, he was reduced to this? She wanted to run to him, but that could earn the both of them a world of pain. He gave a subtle shake of his head as if he could read her thoughts.

Judd raised his diver's knife.

Cora stumbled. "Please, no!"

He frowned at her, then bent down to cut away the ties that bound Kirk's wrists.

"You had us on your boat." Anger burned in Kirk's gaze as he stood and rubbed his wrists. "You were with us in Farrow Village. Protected us when someone shot at us. Why didn't you abduct us then?"

The big man grimaced as if in pain. Crossed his arms in a show of strength. Was that regret in his eyes? Really? "I didn't want you involved. Okay, man? We were buddies still. I owed you. Lance wanted Cora. She saw something. Eventually she would remember. I had hoped you would lose her and be left to your investigation alone. You wouldn't have found anything. Cora's the one who caused all this. She and Trip got nosy. When she showed up to the dead drop unexpectedly, that started the domino effect. But you...you could have survived this and walked away."

Lance stepped onto the deck, wiping his hands with a towel. His features appeared pale and sweat beaded his brow as he winced. His gunshot wound? "Yeah, well, we obviously didn't agree on that. I wanted the both of you dead. But since you just wouldn't die, I have a better use for you."

Maybe that explained why someone had shot at them while on the island. Lance and Judd disagreed.

"Brothers," Kirk said. "I learned the truth, but I'm not sure how I missed that to begin with."

"I've never gone by Verone and used the surname Maier, and for good reason, as you can see. Judd and I wouldn't be tied together so easily."

"Mind if I ask how a guy working on a research vessel gets involved in something like this and drags his brother down with him?" Kirk eyed Judd. "Because I'm sure Judd wouldn't stoop to this on his own. I know you too well, buddy."

Cora grimaced inside. How could he even still use that term when it came to Judd? But then, Kirk could be trying to play on Judd's sense of right and wrong. Recalibrate his moral compass and then his sympathies. If he had any left.

Judd grunted. "I didn't have a lot of options left to me after the navy. You made it. You'd found a way to survive. I had a hard time finding a job and making a living. Fishing wasn't cutting it. Lance, here, he had a decent job and the perfect cover for us to organize the transfer of products and information. As the ROV pilot, Lance can find the box and maneuver without anyone being the wiser."

"Shut up," Lance said. "He doesn't need to know anything."

"Sure he does. He's my friend. Or, at least, he was. I don't deserve his friendship now."

All his testing and fixing and breaking of the ROV made perfect sense now. All the late nights trying to improve its capabilities.

Lance crossed his arms and stood in a wide stance. "I *was* in the right position. I'm not an ROV operator anymore. There's no ROV on this vessel, or hadn't you noticed? Our connection wants us to up our game and transfer bigger-stakes items now, and doesn't care that the *Sea Dragon* is lost to us and that we don't have all the equipment we need to make it happen smoothly."

"There are a lot easier ways to do this. You know that, right?" Kirk quirked a brow.

"We used the tools available to us. Answered the proposition when it came."

"When you say they want you to transfer bigger-stakes items, do you mean military secrets or something else?"

Like they'd read in Drake's files. Had they already

transferred something of that magnitude, or was that what they planned to do—and that kind of devastating data transfer hadn't been made yet?

"That's enough." Lance busied himself preparing scuba equipment. "Who tipped you off to us?"

"You mean why was I on board working undercover? I didn't know about any of this, but I suspected something. I was here to find out what happened to Drake."

Lance swore.

Cora faced Lance. "You killed him, didn't you? Just like you killed Trip."

"I regret having to get rid of either of them, but they gave me no choice."

Emboldened by his response, she continued, "And you blew up the *Sea Dragon*? Why?"

Lance closed in on Cora and ran his hand down her cheek. "So beautiful. Drake ruined everything for us."

She shuddered.

Kirk grimaced. Why didn't he say anything? But the look in his eyes told her everything—he didn't want to push Lance to harm her more because of him.

Lance dropped his hand. "I had to make you and agent man go away. Destroy the evidence so we could start again. The thing is, we still have something to pick up, the delivery already made. We're behind schedule as it is. And, in case you haven't noticed, agent man here shot me. Coburn isn't any good on a dive now. So we need someone to retrieve it."

Her heart rate jumped. "Are you crazy? I'm not getting drugs for you."

"You're right. You're not." He zeroed his gaze in on Kirk. "Agent man is. He and Judd will do it together."

"What makes you think I'll do it?" Kirk asked.

Lance yanked Cora to him and pointed a pistol at her head.

As Kirk geared up for the dive, he tried to avoid looking at Cora. But then he couldn't resist and stopped everything.

He glanced her way, wishing none of this was happening.

Cora stared out across the sea, refusing to even look at him. He didn't blame her.

Lance kept her close, his gun ready to use. Aim, fire and shoot the woman Kirk could have loved. Might still love. But what was the point now?

He truly was a disappointment, just like he'd believed. No matter how hard he fought to overcome it, the truth was out now.

He'd let her down. Asked her to trust him. Promised to protect her. Jackson had counted on him to find out what happened to Drake, and now the man would never know, because Kirk had failed. He'd managed to disappoint everyone, including himself. He'd wanted Jackson's approval so badly that he sent Cora on her way by herself, and he'd taken the time to read the diary—sure he had his excuses, his justifications for reading that before accusing Drake of being involved—when all he had to do was go with Cora to Seattle and turn in everything he'd found.

He'd wanted so desperately to be a hero, to erase the stigma of feeling like he was always a disappointment, that he'd risked it all.

Risked and lost. He saw that now.

Because of his stupidity, he and Cora would both die at the hands of these criminals.

Judd shoved him enough to get his attention. "What's the matter with you, man? Finish gearing up."

Suddenly, Cora rushed to him. Wrapped her arms around him and whispered in his ear.

"I believe in you, Kirk! Please... I don't want to be lost forever. I don't want my story, our story, to die at the bottom of the ocean."

"Get back here!" Lance snatched her away.

She was definitely looking at him now with hope. Determination.

Everyone he'd ever disappointed faded away.

God, help me. I can get us out of this. I know I can, with Your help.

He didn't know how yet, but deep inside, he knew that something would come to him. The right moment would present itself. This wasn't about him making others happy. Finding the answers Jackson wanted. Making his family proud despite the fact he hadn't become a lawyer. This wasn't even about seeing admiration in Cora's eyes, though her words to him now had lit the fire in him. They were the words he'd needed to hear.

This was about being the best he could be and trusting God that it would be enough.

He finished gearing up, determined to find a way out of this for himself and for Cora. Sweet, beautiful Cora.

He donned his mask. "I'm ready when you are." After he positioned his regulator he rolled back into the cold, dark waters of the Salish Sea.

He must have taken Judd by surprise because seconds ticked by before the man followed. Once in the water, Judd peered at him, suspicion in his eyes. That, along with a hefty dose of regret. Judd didn't want to be in this position. Transporting drugs was one thing, but when lives were at stake—his friend's life in particular—Judd was miserable. This went against everything he believed in.

How did you think it would end, man?

Kirk would use Judd's regrets to his advantage if he could. And if he couldn't, then Judd was dispensable. *Sorry, buddy.*

The good guys had to survive. *Cora* had to survive.

And Kirk, well, he would give his life to make sure that she got out of this alive. That she lived to tell Drake's story.

He followed Judd. This would be a deep dive to find the box at the location given. Once it was found, they would bring down a basket to transport the drugs.

Think, Kirk, think.

They were using Cora against him—which had always been his fear—to ensure his cooperation. But if he didn't find a way out of this, they were both dead anyway.

If Lance was diving with him now, he wouldn't think twice about trying to take the guy out. But it was Judd, his old navy buddy. His heart ripped at the idea of taking out someone he'd cared about. Except Judd had betrayed him in the worst kind of way.

He let that anger, along with Cora's words to him, fuel him to do what had to be done. Those words had zinged right to his heart.

I believe in you, Kirk! Please... I don't want to be lost forever. I don't want my story, our story, to die at the bottom of the ocean.

Still, facing off with the man would be no easy task. Judd was twice Kirk's size and had all the same skills. Kirk couldn't overpower him with brute strength, even underwater.

So how did he get them out of this?

They descended slowly until they found a rusted hull covered in barnacles. With his flashlight, Judd waved for Kirk to go inside the hull ahead of him.

Kirk slowly swam through the water while looking for his way out. Searching for whatever they were supposed to find.

But he saw nothing inside the hull and paused, waiting for Judd. The big man brushed at the sand and clouded up the water. When it settled, a gray box appeared.

The triangular symbol on the box. Trigon.

This was it.

The others dropped off whatever they would leave in the predesignated location and would come back to retrieve their payment in whatever form. Cash or drugs. And in the case of drugs, obviously this was just another way to transport them. Every kind of method had been tried and used, from small submarines to crates of bananas with drugs stuffed inside the peels.

But the end game here had nothing at all to do with smuggling drugs and everything to do with selling technological or military secrets via the transfer of large amounts of data.

Kirk glanced at Judd. He needed to do something to get them out of this. If he could take Judd out when it was just him against one man, then he would have the advantage of surprising the small crew above them.

Judd drew his attention and gestured.

Kirk read his expression clearly enough. *I'm watching you!*

Then Judd motioned for Kirk to open the box. His heart thundered when he needed to remain calm and breathe the compressed air steadily. He removed the latch and opened the box to find what appeared to be white powder secured in waterproof bags. Nausea erupted in his gut.

The box was too heavy for him to lift by himself and dump the contents, but Judd would need Kirk's help to secure it in the basket, which the crew up top were already lowering.

He wanted to ask Judd what they did with the drugs from here? Who was their buyer? And who was leaving this for them?

Following Judd's lead, Kirk assisted him in positioning the box near the basket, then transferring the drug packages into the basket. Why not just put the whole box in the basket?

When they were done, he learned the answer.

They positioned the box back inside the wreck's hull. Judd removed a small waterproof package from his suit. The USB drive containing data?

Kirk couldn't allow the transfer of those secrets. They could eventually cost lives. American lives. He grabbed the basket and smashed it into Judd's head.

His friend floated. Dazed? Unconscious? Dead? Kirk didn't know. He grabbed the drive and removed Judd's diver's knife. He started to cut the man's regulator hose. Or he could kill him with the knife quickly.

Judd's eyes were closed, and blood seeped into his mask.

No. He couldn't be so ruthless. So brutal. But he

would swim away to save Cora. He had minutes, if not seconds, to win their freedom.

He turned to swim away with the USB drive.

Judd grabbed his leg.

TWELVE

Everyone seemed to have forgotten her while they stared over the railing, anxiously waiting for the aluminum basket to be filled with drugs—their payment for secrets.

Was this treason? She supposed it depended on the secrets. Somehow, she and Kirk had to stop them.

"What's taking so long?" Lance growled as he paced. Scraped his hand through his hair. Why hadn't his job operating the ROV, searching for history in the ocean depths, been enough for him? What could drive someone to do such evil things? And where were Scott and Chuck, if not on this boat? Dead? Alive? Or had they had enough and fled, escaping their connection with Lance, Judd and Coburn?

And what about the others? Shari—the medic had to be innocent. *God, please let Shari be okay.*

Coburn eyed the horizon through black binoculars. "We should have waited until dark like we usually do. We're too exposed out here."

"Not this time," Lance said. "The lights could give us away and then we'd be more exposed, stupid."

The tension between them was thick and to be expected when it came to the relationship between these two murderous traitors.

Who were they hiding from? Were the authorities onto them?

They were nervous. She searched the waters, too. The boat was so far out in the Salish Sea, she couldn't make out the island. She doubted anyone knew where they were.

God, please let someone find us here. She couldn't imagine how they could get out of this one.

Even if there was another boat on the water, they would never know she needed help unless she figured out how to send a distress signal.

Getting on the radio and yelling "Mayday!" was definitely out. She didn't have access to the distress button on the radio, either—or red flares to burn, distress rockets to launch or orange smoke to release from a canister. Maybe she could light the boat on fire. Yeah, that would do it. But any signal she could send would also be obvious to their abductors. There were so many options, none of which worked in the case of being abducted and held captive on a boat.

Oh, God, please... I need an idea. I need some way to help!

She'd put entirely too much pressure on Kirk to save the day. He was a protector and, yeah, he was her hero. She would never doubt him again, but he could use her help now. She'd seen the fear in his eyes. And yet she knew he would face that fear head-on. Somehow, someway, down in the depths, he would face off with Judd. And she had to do her part. If she couldn't do anything else, Cora could at least fortify Kirk.

And...there was one more thing she could do...

Slowly she crept to the wall supporting the helm. There she'd have her choice of weapons for use underwater, but she could make do with them. She had no intention of ending up floating lifeless in the water or at the bottom of the ocean should they decide to weigh her body down. Images of shipwrecks with skeletons—the remains of those who'd died—drifted to mind.

She shoved the gruesome images away.

Lance still had a weapon. Once she grabbed the pneumatic speargun, she'd probably have to shoot him. Kill him. Could she do it?

Could she actually *kill* another human being?

Then there was Coburn. He was just looking for a reason to inflict harm on her. He'd probably been the one shooting at them all along—with Lance's approval, of course. The man was bloodthirsty.

With him waiting for the chance to hurt her—if she took this step, she'd have to finish it.

So far, neither of the men was paying attention to her. They both probably thought she was powerless to protect herself. That seemed strange, given that Lance had been the one to encourage her in underwater target practice with the speargun.

Cora kept her pace nice and slow. She stood in one place, arms crossed, for an eternity before inching another step closer to the weapon. It had been hanging there so long it had likely become part of the decorations. Maybe the two men hadn't even noticed. She would have to load the gun quickly or Lance could blow her head off before she could act.

Finally she stood with her back against the wall. Arms crossed, she watched the ocean with Coburn, still praying for help. Like Lance, she wondered what was taking Judd and Kirk so long. Had Kirk gotten the best of Judd? Or vice versa?

Coburn pulled his gaze from the binoculars to look at her. After all, Lance had charged him with the task. Her heart hammered.

Would he see right through her plan?

Was she nuts to even consider it?

A tear threatened to escape. She squeezed her eyes shut. Let him think she was terrified.

And she was.

"Now we're getting somewhere," Lance said. He began the process of returning the basket to the boat.

What? Oh, no. She'd better hurry if she was going to do this. Facing off with Judd along with these men would diminish her chances of success, even with Kirk in the picture.

She took a long, deep breath. Coburn moved to stand next to Lance and peer over the side. Lance would realize Coburn was not watching over her, and he would look in a few seconds. She had to do this.

It was now or never.

Quietly, she maneuvered the pneumatic speargun from where it hung along the wall. Quickly, she grabbed it in the middle with her left hand and, with her right, stuck the spear in. Holding the gun between her knees, she pulled the spear down. She was so glad she'd practiced this repeatedly or she wouldn't have the skills or strength to do it. It took her under fifteen seconds.

She figured she had three seconds left before either of the two men thought to look at her.

She'd made it in time.

Cora held the speargun and aimed it at Lance.

His back was to her, and she realized she couldn't

spear him in the back. Even though she knew he planned to kill her when this was over—and he had already killed her friends—she was weak. A coward.

God, what do I do? What do You want me to do? Killing Lance could save Kirk's life.

And then what about Coburn? She couldn't possibly reload the speargun before Coburn could grab Lance's gun and shoot her.

Back when she'd first come up with the idea, Coburn had been standing on the opposite end of the deck. She could reach the gun before him.

Now what?

Indecision roiled through her.

She took aim at Lance. Her limbs trembled. Lance had once been her friend. What had happened to turn him into this…this monster? Shouldn't she ask him that? Make him listen to reason? Only he'd already committed heinous acts and was too far in to turn back now.

Still, there was always hope.

They hauled the basket aboard. Judd's body rolled out of it.

Cora quietly sucked in a breath. Her pulse roared in her ears.

Lance suddenly stiffened as if he knew something had changed in the atmosphere. Like a shark sensing when it was time to move in—he could smell blood. His own?

He shifted around to look at her and at the same time he whipped his weapon around. They faced off now— each aiming lethal weapons at the other.

He would kill her. She knew it.

His gun went off at the same time she let the spear

fly from the speargun. Cora jerked back as a bullet slammed into her arm, searing her with pain.

Kirk tumbled over the side of the boat near the bow grunting with the effort, feeling the strain of the battle to free himself from Judd. Pain coursed through his heart. He hadn't wanted any of it to end this way He removed the fins, mask and regulator. He crept around, hoping to hit the helm and activate a distress signal, but then he saw Lance sprawled on the deck.

Huh?

Cora screamed.

Kirk ran around the deck to find Coburn pointing a gun at her.

He didn't think. He only acted.

Charging into the man, Kirk sent Coburn crashing into the deck. He wrestled the weapon from his hands and fired it into the boat for a warning shot.

Coburn covered his face. "Okay, man. Okay! But she killed Lance!"

Really? He glanced at Cora, who shivered.

Keeping the weapon on Coburn, Kirk eyed Lance. He crept backward to him and pressed a finger against his carotid. He had no pulse. A spear was thrust through his chest.

Then Kirk's gaze found Cora again. "Cora, honey, you…" Blood. He saw the blood.

He aimed the weapon at Coburn. "Move and I'll kill you."

He rushed to Cora. Fear flayed him. "You're hurt."

Shivering, she squeezed her fingers around her upper arm as blood oozed between them. Her teeth chattered as she spoke. "He…he…shot me. I knew he would so I shot him, too. We shot each other…at the same time."

Kirk was glad she was the better shot, or else she would be lying in a pool of blood. His insides tensed. And with that look on her face, he was worried about her—killing another person was never easy. She was in shock from the gunshot wound and from killing someone. He had to do something. "It's okay, Cora. It was self-defense."

"She was going to shoot him in the back," Coburn yelled. "Lance turned around and she was already pointing that thing at him."

"I wouldn't have shot him, except I knew he would kill me."

"It's all right, Cora. You did the right thing. Let me take care of your arm." He had to secure Coburn before he could be a problem. And he needed to send a distress signal. Or he could take the boat to meet up with the Coast Guard and contact Matt and Jackson, not necessarily in that order.

He shoved all that aside and attended to Cora. "I need to get the first-aid kit. But before I do, I need to secure Coburn so he can't hurt either of us. Are you okay to let me do that?"

"Of course! I was handling it just fine before you got here." She telegraphed to something on the ground.

He followed her gaze and spotted the bang stick—another kind of speargun. She planned to use that on Coburn and kill him. But he had already been there with the gun. Aiming it and ready to fire.

He gripped her arms. "You could have died, Cora. He could have killed you, too." Overcome with more emotion than he could handle, he pulled her to him. "You stayed alive."

"*We* stayed alive." She croaked out the words, reminding him of her injury, as if he could forget. "I've got it. You take care of Coburn. Make sure he doesn't try to hurt us."

"Are you sure you're okay to find the first-aid kit?"

Though visibly shaken, she nodded. He wasn't so sure. "Okay. I'm on Coburn."

Leaning against the wall as she went, she made her way belowdecks.

Kirk marched toward Coburn, who backed away, holding his hands up in surrender. "Whoa…whoa. What are you going to do to me?"

"I'm going to make sure you can't hurt Cora anymore." Kirk eyed the man. He didn't trust him.

"I never hurt her. I didn't…"

"Shut up. You left her for dead. You—" What had happened out there when Cora had nearly drowned? For the first time since this began, he was in a position to get some answers. "Who tried to kill her? Who was the diver out there who tried to kill us when the *Sea Dragon* exploded?"

Coburn vigorously shook his head. "I swear I don't know who it was."

Kirk eyed the gun then flicked his gaze to the man at his mercy, hoping to intimidate him. "Don't make me use this. Or maybe you'd prefer I use the bang stick."

Coburn backed against the deck railing. Would he jump? Why was he so scared? It was like Kirk was the bad guy here. Coburn didn't seem to understand that Kirk wouldn't actually hurt Coburn unless driven to it.

Everything these guys had done over the last months

was so out of character, Kirk didn't know what to make of it. "You were there and saw the whole thing. Tell me everything you know."

"I swear, I didn't know the diver. I didn't recognize him." Coburn thrust his wrists out. "You can tie me up now. I won't fight. I promise."

"What are you so afraid of? Or rather...*who*?"

"I'm not afraid of anyone or anything except for maybe a guy with gun. You have the gun now. I know when I've been beaten. I want to live." Did Coburn really think Kirk would kill him when he was defenseless? Apparently so.

"What do you know about what happened to Drake?"

"He disappeared. I swear that's all I know. I don't know who killed him. I—"

"Kirk." Cora stood next to him, her face pale. Sweat beaded her brow. "I wrapped my arm."

"Oh, honey." He'd taken much too long.

Her nervous gaze scanned the ocean. "We should get out of here. We don't know who else is involved. Maybe the men who left the drugs for these guys to retrieve are still out there waiting and watching. The whole time Lance was waiting for you and Judd to come up, Coburn was looking through his binoculars. I kept hoping he was watching out for the good guys, but I'm not so sure anymore."

"Good point." Maybe that's why Coburn seemed terrified. "Is that right, Coburn? Were you looking for more bad guys?"

Coburn shrugged and held his wrists out again. "Go ahead."

Cora took the gun from Kirk and held it on the man while Kirk tied his wrists.

"Let's take you belowdecks and secure you down there." He let his gaze skim the horizon as a chill crawled over him.

"After I fixed my arm, I sent a distress signal, so someone should respond to that, but doesn't mean we can't keep moving."

Once Coburn was restrained in a stateroom, Kirk returned for Judd. His friend's lids fluttered, then he stared up at Kirk. He was still alive? Guilt suffused him. He should have done more for Judd, but the guy would have thought nothing about killing him, killing Cora, and Kirk had his hands full protecting her against the likes of Coburn.

He reached down to try to heft the guy to his feet. Impossible. The man was dead weight. "Can you give me a little help? I'm taking you belowdecks."

"Why?" Judd's deep voice gurgled. "So you can watch me die? I won't make it that far."

Kirk squatted next to his friend. "I had no choice but to defend myself, Judd. You gave me no choice."

"I didn't want it to be like this. I never wanted it to come to this—you and me fighting on opposite sides."

"Then why?"

"There's more to it. Something you don't understand. I didn't have a choice."

"Then what? Tell me?"

"You're still in danger. I'm…sorry." Judd's eyes glazed over.

Kirk stared at his friend. Gone? He was dead? He shook Judd's shoulders. "No!"

He dropped to his knees next to Judd and dry sobs racked his body. This guy had been almost like a brother to him. Closer than Stephan. That's why his betrayal hurt so much. If he'd had another choice, he wouldn't have fought the guy or stabbed him. Killed him. But it was him or Judd, and he had to think of Cora.

Judd's words, his friend's warning to him, hung in the blood-soaked air.

You're still in danger.

THIRTEEN

Cora sat in the booth in the galley of the *Clara Steele* and kept an eye on Coburn, whom Kirk had secured. She sure hoped Kirk would take them away from this place. She never wanted to be free from anything more than she wanted to be free from these people and this situation.

She popped a couple of ibuprofen from the first-aid kit. Coburn watched her.

"Why'd you do it?" she asked. "Why did any of you do it?"

Coburn hung his head and shrugged. Regret? She wasn't buying it.

"Well? Don't you think I deserve an answer?"

"I don't know why. It started out as a gag, really. Or an adventure. I don't know. Lance asked if I wanted to be in on some spy stuff and make a little extra cash. You know how he is…*was*. Persuasive. Cocky. Always joking, too. I went along with it, but then I was pretty speechless when we brought up a few bags of drugs. Terrified, actually."

She quirked a disbelieving brow, but prompted him to continue.

"Then, a few days later, he gave me a stack of bills. A *big* stack of bills. I thought of a lot of things I could do with that money. Like help my sister attend the private university she couldn't afford. Finally, I could do this for her. I could help. I mean, if it wasn't us doing it, then it would only be someone else. But that was supposed to be it. Just the once."

"But it wasn't just one time, was it?"

"No." He shook his head. "I told Lance no when he approached me again. But he said I was in already and there was no going back. I didn't know what to do." Coburn pressed his face into his hands.

Maybe she'd misjudged him. He'd made a wrong choice and found himself in too deep.

"What about Lance? Why'd he do it?"

"Honestly, I think he didn't have a choice."

Complete hogwash. "How did he get started? Who was his contact?"

"That I really don't know."

She believed him. A chill crept over her and she rubbed her arms. What was taking Kirk so long?

When he stepped into the galley, he looked like he'd just lost his best friend.

Judd...

She hadn't even thought to ask him. Cora rushed to him. "Kirk, is Judd..."

"Dead. He's dead. I killed him."

"I'm so sorry." She wrapped her arms around him. She could have stayed there forever but eased away so she could look up into his eyes. "I'm sure you had no choice. Just like I had no choice but to kill Lance."

His gaze hardened as he set her aside as though he

was afraid to touch her. In two strides he stood in front of Coburn. "Who's behind this?"

"I don't know."

Cora thought Kirk might actually smack the guy. She touched his arm. "I actually believe him."

He worked his jaw.

"Kirk, please." Cora turned him to face her, pulling his attention from Coburn. "We have to get out of here. Don't ask me how I know, it's just a feeling. I mean, unless someone's coming to help us and you see them on the horizon."

"You're right. I'm taking the boat in. We'll turn him over to the authorities—if you're involved in delivering military secrets of the capacity detailed in Drake's files, then the navy will have its way with you."

Coburn's face blanched.

She followed Kirk up top to retrieve the anchor. He peered through the binoculars. "No one's coming. I don't understand. You sent a distress signal."

"Maybe the signal isn't working." She caught Kirk and held his arm until he peered down at her. "We did it. We made it. We survived this. You saved me again." She couldn't stand to see him so distraught and thought to encourage him.

"No. There's much more going on. Judd told me we're still in danger."

"You mean from whoever is behind all this. Whoever approached Lance or Judd and propositioned them."

He nodded, all serious now, and pulled away from her, but squeezed her hand before letting go completely. His reassurance meant everything. She understood it was time to focus and get them out of this. She was glad she was with Kirk—he would get them to safety.

He started the boat and steered toward the Washington coast as the sun set and a few stars began to appear. The wind picked up. Under any other circumstance Cora would have found this romantic. She couldn't imagine anyone else she would want to share that with.

She wanted a second chance with Kirk. But would he want one, too? That is, if they survived this. She hoped their predicament would come to an end soon.

"Ah, the Coast Guard is here." Kirk slowed the vessel to allow them to board. "I almost wish you hadn't sent the distress signal."

"Why not? What are you talking about?"

Gripping her arms, he turned her to face him. "Because I don't know who is behind this. I don't know how to keep you safe."

Emotion swirled in his gaze. She thought she might have preferred the hardness to this fear. "It's going to be okay, Kirk. The Coast Guard—they're the good guys."

"I need you to do me a favor."

"Of course. Anything."

"Tell them about everything except Drake's files. Don't tell them what you learned back there about the diary. Say nothing about military secrets. All you know about is they kidnapped you and wanted us to dive for drugs. Understood?"

Cora nodded her agreement as the shock of what she still faced coursed through her.

Somehow Farrow Island didn't seem nearly so ominous this time, even though it was nearing ten o'clock at night. He stepped onto the boardwalk with Cora after they'd given their statements to the Coast Guard, glad to be back on solid ground after what they'd endured at sea.

Still, Kirk believed this wasn't over yet—at least, it wouldn't be until he'd turned all he knew over to Matt tomorrow, when they were to meet to debrief.

He would be meeting with Commander Jackson after that. The man was already en route from DC.

His boss had been furious that Kirk hadn't followed protocol to begin with when he'd listened to Jackson—who had reassured Kirk he would smooth it over with Matt. Still, Matt had also said that Jackson commended Kirk on a job well done. All this before either of them had all the facts.

The only issue now was that Jackson had wanted to meet with him today. Tonight. It had already been late when the Coast Guard dropped them off on the island. So Kirk had put him off until tomorrow.

He'd bought himself some time by claiming he had to gather the information he'd secured before he could meet with Jackson. Plus, he had to figure out how to tell him the worst of it—that Drake had been involved. Maybe the man already suspected as much, and that's why he'd been eager to agree to let Kirk investigate.

It was like working for two bosses—but the bottom line was that Kirk had been the one to pursue finding out what happened to Drake. Just like that boy they'd found on the beach when they were kids—he'd wanted to find out what had happened to him. In this case, they were still missing the body after several months.

Commander Jackson had been the one to pull strings to get this assignment, and considering someone had leaked that Kirk was undercover, he wasn't sure who he could trust. But he could definitely trust the man who'd given him the assignment and whose son's death he was looking into. So Kirk had been compelled to contact Jackson first when the *Sea Dragon* had been destroyed.

Regardless, he'd happily accept the commendations from Matt and Jackson. He just had to figure out how to make them both happy when he presented the information and his discoveries.

It seemed he was always trying to please others.

So what if he hadn't pursued becoming an attorney like his father and followed in the family business? They had Stephan. He was the one they'd always wanted. It didn't matter they didn't know about his womanizing. Maybe they knew and didn't care. But Kirk had made his own way—with God's help. His own successes.

The village was still hopping at this late hour during the weekend event, but they'd just missed the night-time fireworks display. Cora sighed next to him as they strolled in the moonlight, drawing his attention back to the beautiful woman by his side.

The medic on the cutter had attended to her gunshot wound. Kirk was grateful it hadn't been worse. Regardless, her world had been ripped apart. He wanted to rush her to the ferry again, only this time make sure she was indeed safe, and then take care of his business, but she needed a reprieve. So they strolled and meandered while he figured out his next step.

She looked up at him, her eyes shimmering in the moonlight. His only regret was losing Cora to begin with. He should have fought for her back then—he saw that now. But more than that, he wasn't entirely sure he deserved a chance to win her heart again. He wasn't the hero she now seemed to believe he was. He'd repeatedly failed her through this. Sure he'd saved her multiple times, but she never should have been a target to begin with and that was on him. He should have prevented it.

"What are you thinking about?" she asked.

"I'm glad to have that over with." He took Cora's hand. She didn't resist.

"I don't understand why you wouldn't let me tell them everything."

"Let's just say I have a feeling the navy doesn't want anyone to know someone is stealing their secrets. Plus, Cora—" he slowed and turned her to face him "—the less you know, the safer you'll be."

"You're meeting with your boss tomorrow to debrief. I heard you on the phone."

What else had she heard?

"Is this over or not, Kirk?"

He hesitated. "I can't be sure. Look, I want to put you on that ferry back to Seattle tonight, but I can't forget what happened last time. And this time I don't know the other players. I can't be the one to take you, Cora. It would be best if I hand you off to someone I can trust. There are still a few things I need to take care of here on Farrow."

"You should have let the Coast Guard take me down the coast."

"I don't trust your safety with just anyone. Maybe you could contact one of your sisters to come and pick you up. To escort you home. I know it's late here." Kirk wanted to take her home himself, but he couldn't leave until he was done meeting with Jackson.

"I need a phone for that."

"Here, use this one." He handed over the burner Lance had called him on. He'd managed to retain it.

Together they strolled the boardwalk while she made

the call, his sense of protectiveness growing again. Maybe all the trauma they'd experienced was finally getting to him. Or maybe it was something more. If only he could have relied on someone else to take her back to Seattle, but after trusting Judd with her, with their lives, he'd be hard-pressed to trust anyone again.

"Hello, Jonna? Yes. This is…" Cora's laugh reminded him of happier times. "I'm on Farrow Island. Listen, I can explain later but I need help."

"Yes." She listened. "No. It's…" Cora looked to Kirk. "Can you and Ian come and get me? Oh, sure. I can wait."

Kirk snatched the phone. "You don't know me, but I'm NCIS Special Agent Kirk Higgins. This is a matter of national security and Cora's safety. You and your husband are the only ones I trust her with at this time. When can you get here?"

"Oh, wow," Jonna said. "Sure, we'll be there as soon as possible. Ian has a friend with a small plane. We could fast-track things. But even then, it would still take us a couple of hours. Can I reach you at this number?"

"For now." Guilt suffused him. "I hate getting you and Mr. Brady involved. If there was any other—"

"You don't have to explain. I've been in situations where I don't know whom to trust. Thank you, Agent Higgins, for caring so much about Cora's safety."

"I'll hand the phone back to Cora now."

She took it from him. "Thanks, sis. Please be careful." Cora ended the call. "Wow."

"What is it?"

"It sounds like this really isn't over."

A muscle ticked in his jaw. "I'm not taking any chances."

"Where are we headed now, while we wait?" she asked.

"I left the file and the diary stashed at the internet café next to the ferry terminal. Let's just hope they're still there."

Once inside the café, Kirk tugged Cora behind him and hurried over to the table where he'd been sitting when Lance called him. His gut soured at the memory. They'd taken Cora then, and Kirk had been both furious and terrified they would hurt her. He wasn't sure he could ever forgive himself for putting her in harm's way.

A family sat at the table.

"So what do we do now?" Cora asked.

"We'll wait, and then if it takes too long, I'll be rude and maneuver around them to get what I need."

Cora and Kirk sat at a nearby table.

"I'll get us some coffees," she said.

The bar was a few yards away. "Okay, sure. Make mine black."

He kept an eye on her and the family, hoping they would move quickly—after all, it was pretty late to keep kids up. What did he know? But with two toddlers in tow and a busy blue-eyed, curly-haired little girl, it seemed everything took much longer. An eternity seemed to be ticking by while he waited to get to what he left behind.

To his horror, the little girl started exploring the small opening near the pillar and pulled out the file. "What's this?"

Papers slid onto the floor and fanned out.

FOURTEEN

Cora turned with two hot coffees and witnessed the whole thing.

Kirk exploded onto the scene, frightening the child. He snatched the papers up while the mother grabbed her daughter.

Cora set the coffees on the table. "Oh, here, let me help."

On the floor on all fours, she scooped up the papers. "You get the diary," she whispered.

"What is this?" the little girl asked.

Her mother tried to take the files from Cora, who stood. "I'm sorry but these are top secret files hidden here by my friend who is a special agent. We came to retrieve them. If you don't want your family to be in danger, then you need to leave."

Sometimes the truth sounded ridiculous, but maybe it would have the right effect.

The woman laughed, but Cora remained serious. She held up her arm. "See this? It's a gunshot wound." Then she glanced at the family.

That did it. The mother's face took on a look of horror. "Hank, let's get out of here." After gathering up their things, loading cups in diaper bags and grabbing toys, the family retreated from the café. Cora wondered if they lived on the island or had come for a weekend retreat. If it were the latter, they might never come back.

Kirk approached Cora. "How did you do that?"

"I told her the truth."

"You *what*?"

"Not the details, but enough to scare her into keeping her family safe."

"Good job. Maybe you could consider working for—"

"No, thanks."

They sat at the table previously occupied by the small family. "You don't even know what I was going to say."

"It doesn't matter. Now, get your diary so we can get out of here."

Kirk reached into the tight space—easily accessed by the small child—and pulled out the leather-bound book.

Cora eyed it. "If I hadn't been searching for a weapon in the side table drawers, we wouldn't have the diary. We should read it before you hand it over."

"I read some of it, and I intend to finish it. Just not here."

A man slid into the seat next to Cora. "I'm so glad I found you."

"Commander Jackson," Kirk said. "What are you doing here? Our meeting isn't until tomorrow." *How did you find me?*

"The Coast Guard told me they had dropped you off. I couldn't risk the information you found getting into the wrong hands." He eyed the leather-bound book. "What's that?"

"It's Drake's diary."

The hint of a frown crept over Jackson's forehead then disappeared, but he didn't appear surprised. At all. "You did good, son. I'm so proud of you. I've always thought of you as my own son. You know that."

Satisfaction beamed in Kirk's eyes, along with grief. Understandable. Something else she understood—Kirk needed this affirmation. He'd done all of this for Commander Jackson as much as for himself and the job. He'd done this to find out what happened to Drake and, unfortunately, hadn't liked what he'd found.

"Did you read it?" Jackson asked, referring to the diary.

"I...I hadn't finished."

"Can I have it?"

"You know the protocol. My superior is expecting to debrief, in which case I'll turn this all over to NCIS and then they will hand it on to you."

"Now, son, you wouldn't even be working undercover on this assignment to learn what happened to my son, your best friend, if it weren't for me pulling those strings. I thought we had an agreement between us. I want what belongs to Drake. At least let me read it first, then you can have it back. We can sit right here while I read it."

"Sir, I'm afraid you're not going to like what you read."

Intensity poured off the navy officer and Cora leaned away from him.

"Why is that?" he asked.

"If I may," Cora said.

"Cora, don't." Kirk glared at her.

"I worked with Drake. He was a good man. I read the files and it appeared he was gathering information to take the drug-running participants who traded military secrets down."

Yeah, maybe she'd said too much. But why waste time with this man—a commander in the navy? He would find out sooner or later.

Jackson didn't respond. He didn't even look at her. But he looked at Kirk. "You let her read them?"

"She found them when she was abducted, sir. She found his diary, too."

"So you're not the one to be commended, but rather she is." Jackson's words had to sting Kirk.

Cora felt compelled to stand up for him. "Kirk risked his life a thousand times over for me. If it wasn't for him, you'd never know the truth about what happened to Drake. We wouldn't have the files."

"All the same, I'd like to look at them. I can do that now. We can sit right here. I want to know what you learned about my son. That was our agreement."

"It was, at that." Kirk pursed his lips and pushed the diary and the file folder over.

Jackson took them and opened the leather-bound diary. "I need closure about my son's death. I'm sure you can understand that."

"I do, sir." All the oomph had gone out of Kirk.

Cora wished she could somehow restore it for him, but it didn't work that way. He had to get it back for himself.

Jackson flipped through the pages of the diary, only stopping to truly read a few times, then he shut it and passed it back. "Now you can hand it over to your superior, but I don't think they'll need it. There's no mention of Trigon."

Cora's pulse soared for no reason she could fully understand. Then it hit her…and Jackson, too. His face was the one to pale this time.

He and Kirk studied each other, both unwilling to speak.

Jackson swiped at the file and made to stand.

"I never told you about Trigon, sir." Kirk stood and pressed a fist into the file on the table, preventing the commander from taking it.

"No, I suppose you didn't." Jackson pressed a gun against Cora's rib cage.

Kirk's heart cracked and a cold chill blasted through him unlike anything he'd felt before. Jackson was the naval officer passing the secrets. How could Kirk have been such an idiot? "I thought of you like a father, just like you said you thought of me like a son. Drake was my best friend when we were kids. So, for my sake, please let her walk away. There's no need to involve Cora."

Kirk kept trusting the wrong people. Why hadn't Drake mentioned his father in his notes? Was it possible that he didn't know Commander Jackson was the contact? Or had he suspected him and had been trying to prove his suspicions wrong?

Jackson frowned, appearing to regret the words he had to say. "Like it or not, son, she's already in the middle of this. Bring the file and the diary. Both of you are coming with me. Try anything and I'll kill Cora. It's obvious that you care for her."

Her brows were deeply furrowed as she flicked her gaze to him. Kirk expected to see utter disappointment there, but instead saw something else. Confidence. Trust. He read them plainly in her eyes.

Come on, Kirk. You've got this.

If only he could believe in himself the way she appeared to believe in him. Or was he delusional?

How did she expect him to get them out of this? With Jackson holding Cora tightly to him, the gun pressed into her side, Kirk wouldn't risk trying to get the upper hand.

Jackson led them to an alley behind the café where a black sedan with dark windows waited.

"Open the trunk," Jackson demanded.

Cora did as he asked.

Kirk was helpless to do anything at the moment. But he had to find a way out of this. Whatever it took, he would save Cora again and end this once and for all.

"Now, you get in the trunk." Kirk followed the man's instructions.

Jackson stood far enough back to ensure that Kirk couldn't relieve him of the weapon he continued to hold on Cora. Jackson squeezed her injured arm, probably hoping to solicit a cry from her, and definitely to warn Kirk.

To Cora's credit, though her face appeared pained, she kept silent.

He caught her gaze and held it. *Don't worry, honey. I'm going to get us out of this. I always do.*

While she wasn't a mind reader, he hoped she understood him on some deep level. He hoped she understood that he would do anything to protect her because she meant the world to him. Nothing was more important to him.

Once Kirk was inside, Jackson made to close the trunk but reached in. Kirk saw the gun coming his way and tried to move, but Jackson was too fast.

Everything went black.

* * *

Someone kept hitting his head with a hammer. Kirk moaned and tried to move away. But it was no use. The hammer was inside his head.

"Kirk, you're awake," a familiar voice whispered.

He knew that voice. He treasured that voice. "Cora…" He peeled his eyes open to see a dimly lit bedroom. They were situated on the bed, tied back-to-back.

"Where are we?"

"Drake's house. Or, at least, the house that held the files. We're in one of the bedrooms."

"What else can you tell me?"

"I'm pretty sure we're going to die." Her voice quavered. "I think he's going to burn the house down."

"Yeah, I smell the gasoline." That would lead investigators to believe it was arson, but only if anyone thought to investigate. Jackson could have the power to nix that. With the house gone, the files and diary, too, and Kirk and Cora dead, anyone who could tell the full story would be gone.

If only Cora had shared something with the Coast Guard. If only Kirk had told Matt anything of what he'd found, something he'd planned to do in his debriefing tomorrow.

"Let's see if we can maneuver off this bed. Then we can find something to cut our ties and go out the window."

"Um… The windows are boarded over. It won't be that simple."

"You've had some time to think about this."

"Yes. I was worried about you. It took you a long time to wake up. I—I thought he'd killed you." Her voice was thick with emotion *Goddard* how's your head?"

"It's been better. Cora... I..."

"What, Kirk? Please tell me."

"I don't know if you feel the same, but I want you to know you mean everything to me. I'm going to get us out of this—" *God willing* "—and then..."

"We can talk about what happens next once we're free because you're right, we're getting out of this. And, Kirk, I feel the same. It's...always been you."

Despite the grim circumstances, he grinned. "Now that we've got that settled, let's get out of here."

He tried to shimmy toward his side of the bed. "You coming with me?"

"Sure. Let's do this."

"Cora."

"Yeah?"

"I'm sorry I got you into this."

"It's like the navy commander guy said, I was already in the middle of it. I started the whole thing when I became suspicious and decided to investigate. If you hadn't been there, I would have died after the first attack without anyone being the wiser. Maybe that's what happened to Drake."

A wave of grief welled up inside him. "That's what I'm thinking."

"And we'll never find his remains. His story *will* be told, though. We'll make sure of it."

"Perhaps, if the navy allows it. It could all be classified when this is over."

She frowned. "I hadn't thought of that."

"Another reason why I didn't want you telling anyone what you knew."

Distress ~~s~~ ~~uo~~ his back.

They rolled off.

"Ow!" ~~Okay~~?"

"Sure, that just hurt my arm. Now what do we do?"

Kirk had tried to protect her from the fall. "See if we can get to our feet."

"That's not going to be easy."

"I'll take the burden of it, since I weigh more than you."

"And you're stronger."

His lips quirked. "I don't know. You're pretty strong."

"But you have a lot of muscle, Kirk."

The way she said it, he thought he might just blush—and he wasn't a blushing kind of guy—but no time for that. "We have to hurry."

With a grunt and a shove, he forced them onto their feet. He could already smell smoke. Not good. The boarded window could be their only way out of this.

"Something's not right," she said.

"You think?"

"No need to be sarcastic. I mean, Jackson had meant to poison us, or make us sleep somehow, so that when the house burned up it would look like we'd slept together and died in a fire. He didn't want you waking up."

"How do you know this?" he asked.

"He told me."

"Well, he must have changed his mind."

"And that could mean there's a way for us to get out of this, which doesn't make sense." Cora coughed.

"It doesn't matter right now. I can't remove the boards without free hands. Let's look for something on the dresser or in the drawers."

"There," she said. "I see something."

He glanced her way. "What is it?"

"Nail clippers."

He didn't want to give up but at the moment, he was out of ideas. He could care less if anyone was disappointed. He just wanted to save Cora. Maybe he wanted to save himself, too. If they survived this, he vowed to work up the nerve to ask her to dinner. To try again.

God, please help us out of this. I don't have to be the hero, after all, I promise. Send someone else to help, but please save us.

Heat penetrated the walls. The fire crackled on the other side of the door as paint bubbled on the walls.

"I'm not ready to die!" Cora cried.

Her words shattered his already cracked heart.

FIFTEEN

Oh, Lord, I can't believe it's come to this. Jonna and Sadie are going to be so upset with me. And poor Kirk, please save him. Save us.

"I have an idea." Kirk coughed, his voice hoarse.

"I'm all ears." She wished her hands were free so she could protect her mouth and nose from the smoke.

"I want you to keep working on these ropes," he said. "You're the expert with knots. Keep trying to get your hands free."

"I haven't stopped trying." Nor had she made much progress. "Is that your big idea?"

"No. This is the same room we were in before. The window is boarded because it was the one broken when I exchanged gunfire with Lance."

"So? I fail to see how that makes any difference."

"I had to practically climb the wall to get into that window. The way the house is situated on the mountain, it's a decent distance off the ground, a bigger drop on this side." He shimmied them over to the boarded window. "Which would mean the nails were driven in from the inside, not the outside."

"Kirk. Who cares? Smoke will overcome us soon."

She hacked. "I didn't do that on purpose to emphasize my point."

He positioned them sideways.

"What are you doing?" Smoke began to filter beneath the door. "Shouldn't we crouch close to the ground and stay low or something?"

In reply, he simply grunted. Seconds ticked by, then he said, "I'm using those fingernail clippers to see if I can remove the nails."

"Oh, please." Her knees might just give out. That would get them nowhere.

Fire was the absolute worst death she could think of. Drowning didn't come close to burning.

"Cora, please hold still. Hold me up. Help me if you can."

"I'm sorry. You're right." He was trying. At least he was trying.

"There, I got one nail out."

She eyed the door. At this rate, it wouldn't be enough.

"I know what you're thinking," he said. "And you're right."

He was a mind reader, was he? "Don't give up, Kirk. We have to keep trying. You're doing great. Keep working on the nails."

"I have another idea," he said.

"A better one, I hope."

"We're going for a walk."

She maneuvered with him as best as she could.

"There's a brass lamp. Just like the one you used on Coburn."

"Is that your idea? What am I supposed to do with that? Do you want me to bash through those boards? That's not going to happen." Unless…wait.

The ropes dropped from her hands. "Kirk, I did it! I freed my hands." Now they were getting somewhere!

They just might have a chance!

"Great, now untie mine."

She did as he asked, but it was much more complicated—she knew because she had been the one to tie the knot.

"What's taking so long?"

"Um…it's a constrictor knot. It can be impossible to untie."

"Oh, great."

"It's a good knot, what can I say?"

He huffed. "You couldn't have just faked it?"

"No, Jackson was watching. He threatened to kill you if I didn't secure you so you couldn't get out. I was trying to save your life."

"So that I could just die later because of your impossible-to-untie knot?"

The ropes slid away. "Okay. I'm done."

He twisted around and stared at her. "Cora, you're amazing."

Without wasting another second, Kirk worked on the nails.

Cora grabbed sheets from the bed and stuffed them under the door. She kept the pillowcases to cover their faces if needed. "That should slow the smoke though it's already intolerable in this room."

He huffed, sweat pouring from his face and soaking his shirt. "The nails are out."

But nothing happened.

"Then why is the board still there?"

"It's wedged in. I can't get purchase with my fingers. I'll use the lamp." He wedged the base between the board and the window, and then leveraged it until the board popped out.

"You did it!" She jumped into his arms.

He embraced her in return and pressed his face in her neck as if to breathe her in. If only they could stay like this forever.

Then he released her. "Now we have to climb out, and it won't be easy. But at least we have a chance."

An explosion rocked the house. Cora screamed as the ceiling came down on them.

Kirk threw himself over Cora to protect her from the falling debris. Heat flashed over his body. Flames licked at them from everywhere. They had to get out of this house.

"Cora, let's go! We'll just have to risk the jump."

But Cora didn't reply. She didn't move.

She was limp beneath him. "Cora?"

He searched for a pulse and found it. Relief whooshed through him. He'd done his best to protect her, but it hadn't been good enough. The force of the blast as he covered her body must have caused her to hit her head. Now they both would sport a knot and a concussion. What did it matter if they didn't escape? He lifted her into his arms. Escaping would be more difficult now, but he could do it. He had minutes, if not seconds, to get them out.

He found the marine rope she'd used to tie him up, retrieving a long strand, long enough to use to climb out of the window. He tied it to the heavy four-poster bed, then put her body over his shoulder in a fireman's hold. With Cora on his shoulder, he eased through the window, then climbed down the side of the house until the rope ran out. Kirk let go and dropped to the ground, careful he didn't allow Cora to fall.

Once on the ground he had to be careful they didn't continue to roll down the slope. He repositioned her in his arms, then carried her away down the hill and away from the burning house. Chunks of debris still rained down from the explosion. Jackson had seriously rigged it. He'd effectively destroyed all the evidence.

Considering all the trouble he'd gone to, the man was not going to stop until Kirk and Cora were dead—they were the only witnesses to his crimes, except Coburn who knew nothing about Jackson's involvement. Or, at least, he claimed he knew nothing. Kirk didn't know what had happened to Scott and Chuck. Jackson might not know that Coburn or the others were ignorant of his involvement. He might risk having Coburn murdered for what he did know.

All of it could somehow link back to Jackson.

Was that what this had all been about? When Kirk had come to Jackson wanting to find out what had happened to Drake, Jackson had planted Kirk on the vessel to find out what was going on. Not only to find out what happened to Drake and who had been complicit in his death, but to learn who *all* the players were. Jackson would destroy them all, if necessary.

He had almost accomplished that task.

How had Jackson even met Lance and conceived the idea to use the ROV?

Or had it all come through Judd? Yes, that was it. Judd had been navy. Jackson could have held something over his buddy…some dark secret that could get him court-martialed.

Kirk tromped through the woods, everything becoming so much clearer now. Everything except the why. Why would Jackson stoop to selling secrets?

Kirk's legs and back throbbed and burned from the exertion and the blast. He found a dense copse of trees and sat down in the thick of it for cover, Cora still in his arms. He cradled her on his lap, hoping she would wake up soon, come out of this alive. Having saved her so many times only to lose her now was unthinkable.

He brushed his thumb over her smudged cheek. "Wake up, Cora."

Please, God.

Her long lashes fluttered. Hope rose in his chest.

She squinted up at him. "What happened?"

Cora tried to move away but he held her tight. He couldn't bear to let her go.

"The house exploded. Imploded. Something. The roof caved in. We were near the window so the wall support beams kept us from being crushed, but you hit your head."

She reached around and found the knot. He knew because she winced.

"You probably have a concussion. We'll get you to a doctor to be examined as soon as possible."

"Seems like this is where it all started. Me waking up with you watching. Me needing to see a doctor. Except…well…when I woke up before, I wasn't in your arms."

He tucked her tighter. Why couldn't they just stay like this forever, hidden away in the woods where nobody could find them and hurt them?

"You can let me go now."

He grinned. "Why are you so eager to be free of me?"

The hint of a smile inched onto her lips. He could

see it because the house fire lit up the night. Fire truck sirens rang out in the distance. Likely the volunteer fire department had seen the smoke.

"I'm not eager to be free of you. But tell me this— is it finally over?"

"Not unless Jackson died in the house fire."

Her eyes widened and she gasped. "I heard voices in the house while you were still out. An argument of some kind. Whoever argued with him could still be in the house."

She broke free and stood, as if she would run back.

He jumped to his feet and caught her. "Hold on. You can't go into the house. Besides, Jackson could be waiting and watching to make sure it's all done."

A twig snapped. He pulled her to him. More footfalls resounded, then a figure stepped into their hidden copse.

"I thought I'd never find you."

Drake?

SIXTEEN

"Drake Jackson." Unsteady on his legs at the sight of his childhood best friend, Kirk nearly stumbled. Relief whooshed through him. He could hardly believe he was looking at Drake in the flesh. But how? "You're still alive. How is that possible? Everyone thought you were dead. Thinks you're dead. Even your father. Lance admitted to killing you." And Kirk had thought he was guilty. Was he?

"Lance left me for dead. I should be dead but I survived. I thought I should lay low and see what more I could find out, especially after learning my father was involved."

A heaviness edged his tone.

"Where is your father now?" Kirk kept himself in a defensive stance. He couldn't trust anyone, not even Drake. Not yet.

"Dead. We argued. I wanted to save you. To free you. The house was burning down around us and he was trying to get us both out when it exploded. Debris fell down on him and…crushed him."

Drake slowly sat on a protruding tree root and hung his head. "I made it out. I thought you were goners, too, but then I saw someone in the shadows fleeing the house. I hoped I'd find you."

Drake lifted his gaze to meet Cora's and then Kirk's. "I'm so sorry you had to get dragged into this."

"I don't understand why you would be involved in something like this," Kirk said. "You're not the guy I knew growing up."

Though sorrow and grief filled Drake's eyes, he chuckled. "I'm working undercover for CGIS, Kirk. Drug smuggling on the high seas is our jurisdiction. I just didn't expect to learn that my father—a commander in the navy—was committing treason."

Drake hung his head and fisted his hands in his hair. Kirk understand that emotion, the anguish. He wanted to do the same thing.

"I'm guessing he didn't know you were on the research vessel."

"No. Not at first. The dead drops had been ongoing. I planted myself there and was making headway in gathering intel when Lance found out."

"I still don't get why you didn't come forward and tell someone you were alive." Then Kirk would never have joined the research vessel and the last few weeks—and hours—would have been very different.

But then he wouldn't have met Cora again.

She would have been far safer, far better off. The *Sea Dragon* would still be functioning and the guilty parties arrested, and Cora would still be conducting her research, looking for undocumented shipwrecks. Working at the job of her dreams unfazed by the criminal acts of these traitors.

"I was recovering from multiple knife wounds in a small hospital on Lopez Island—the next island over.

I gave them an alias. Said I lived on the island and had no family or friends. I was on my own. I couldn't have Lance or someone else learning I was laid up. And I didn't know how my father would react."

Kirk's jaw flexed and his fists clenched at his sides. "Well, now you do. He sent me to investigate what happened to you, all because of him. Why didn't he just stop with the dead drops or make other arrangements?"

"Once there was momentum, exchanges made, he couldn't so easily stop. He couldn't so easily establish connections and transfer points. Not with someone else—his connection—holding treason over his head. Holding out on payments, if needed."

"Any idea why he would do this?" Cora asked.

"Even as a commander in the navy, his salary was barely six figures. He was facing bankruptcy. A bankruptcy would interfere with his security clearance and he was a mover and shaker on some big projects. That's the way I see it."

"And yet he would share military secrets." That made no sense to Kirk. Maybe the man hadn't intended for things to go so far or to get in so deep, and then it had been too late.

"It didn't start out like that. But once he was in he couldn't get out. He was blackmailed to keep giving more."

"Do we know who he was delivering the information to?" Kirk asked.

"Levi-Saraf. A pro-Russian separatist from Crimea with Canadian citizenship. These waters are along the Canadian border. It's easy to dive and swim beneath the surface to deliver the goods and retrieve the data from a dead drop in a shipwreck, given the *Sea Dragon*'s legitimate stops, or other specific locations. Cash or drugs were left behind. Judd and Lance used connections to make appropriate exchanges and also make sure my father's cut was delivered to him. Judd had no choice."

"I figured that much. Your father blackmailed him somehow."

"Yes. While still in the navy, Judd extracted his own justice after someone attacked his girlfriend. He could have been court-martialed but my father made it go away and yet held it over his head." Drake pushed to his feet. "It sounds like the fire trucks and the authorities have finally made their way to save the day."

"The house is yours," Kirk said.

"No. It's a friend's. She's been in Missouri with her sick mother. I was using it for a home base while working on the *Sea Dragon*. Now I'll have to call her and tell her what happened."

"A friend?"

Drake's mouth twitched. "Okay, she's more than that."

"And she knew you were alive?"

"Maybe."

Kirk rose to his feet. He drew Drake into a bear hug. "I'm sorry about your dad, man. I…couldn't believe it when I found out, either." He released Drake, then said, "I'm glad to know we're on the same team." He hoped. He prayed. But he wasn't counting on it.

Kirk wanted to believe Drake. But he couldn't truly know if Drake was telling him the truth. It could all be a ruse.

"It's time to hand over the USB drive, Kirk."

Drake's audacity took Kirk by surprise. Then again, if he were making up his CGIS position, Kirk should expect him to ask for the drive. If Kirk didn't give it to him, he could try to take it.

"What USB drive?"

Drake rolled his eyes and held out his hand. "Come on. I know you have it."

"How do you know?"

Cora looked at Kirk, surprise and a question in her eyes. She hadn't known he had it, either.

So how could Drake?

"Because you wouldn't have come this far without getting your hands on that drive that contains the information."

Kirk pointed his gun at Drake. "You're not working CGIS, are you?"

Drake held up his hands. "I swear. You can turn me in and I'll prove it to you."

"How do you know I have the drive?"

"Because I was watching you in the internet café with a pair of binoculars. I saw you palm it and tuck it away. How do you think I knew my father had taken you? How do you think I knew to look for you here? I watched the whole thing and followed you here where I confronted him." His voice cracked.

Learning about his father's crimes hadn't been easy on him.

Kirk hesitated, not convinced. "I want to trust you, but I thought I could trust Judd. He betrayed me in the worst possible way."

"That's understandable."

"Why do you need the drive?" Kirk narrowed his eyes at his friend. "So you can deliver it to Levi-Saraf? I don't think so. That flash drive stays with me. I'm going to give the drive to my boss at NCIS tomorrow."

Drake laughed. He actually laughed. "I think what's going on here is a turf war. Fine, I concede. You're the one to get the drive so you can keep it. You can be the hero. How'd you do it, anyway?"

Kirk sighed, but never lowered his weapon. "I had to take Judd out."

"No way."

Cora nodded. "He did."

"And Cora took out Lance with a speargun."

"That's what Lance gets for teaching you everything you needed to know just so he could get close to you and charm his way into your life."

"I didn't want to kill him, Drake." Sorrow laced her words.

Kirk wanted to go to her and comfort her, but he had to remain guarded, even around Drake.

"I'm sorry. You're right. Listen, Kirk, I appreciate that you're not sure you can trust me, and it does hurt a little, but at least let me pull out my credentials. I have them on me now because I was going to reveal that I was alive and turn in what I knew. Everything I'd learned. Just so you know—my superior, Gage Sessions, knows that I'm alive."

Cora gasped and shared a look with Kirk.

Carefully, Drake slid a wallet out of his pocket and tossed it over. Kirk gestured to Cora. She opened it. "Yeah, it says he's CGIS. I recognize this. I've seen Gage's badge."

"Call him up, if you don't believe me. He'll vouch for me."

Finally, Kirk relented, lowering his weapon. "I don't have to. But I *am* keeping the USB drive."

He hoped no one else knew he had it or where they were. It was dangerous to hold on to it.

"Fine. NCIS can have it then. And if you don't mind, I'll call Gage to let him know what's happened." He grinned though he'd lost this particular battle and pulled out his cell. He stared at it as if looking for a signal before making a call.

Cora moved closer to Kirk then slipped her arms around him. "I'm glad you have your friend back. This is good, Kirk. This is a better outcome than you could have ever imagined."

He tugged her tighter. "You're right. It is." And he'd found Cora again. He was ready to start something new with her. He'd dared to hope he'd have this chance, if only they could survive. Well they had, and now was the time to make his move. He turned her to face him and lifted her chin. "There's something I've been wanting to ask you when this was over."

"Yeah? What's that?"

"Will you have dinner with me?"

"Sure, but I'm kind of disappointed."

Oh. Kirk hated that word. He started to step away.

Cora didn't let go. "I was hoping you would ask me for a kiss."

"Cora, can I kiss you?"

"Do you even have to ask?" she winked.

He grinned and pressed his lips against hers, breathing in the essence that was Cora. His hands holding her head, cherishing her, he wrapped her silky hair in his fingers as he urged her lips closer, feeling their softness, embracing the emotion that poured from her, while giving back all that he could. All that he was. This moment, this kiss with her after the battle, was more than he could have hoped for.

"Okay. I'm glad to see that the guy gets the girl, but we need to get going now." Of course Drake would try to interrupt. This wasn't *his* movie scene.

But Kirk ignored him and thoroughly kissed Cora, he hoped, until her head was spinning. He could do this forever, and hoped it would end differently this time.

Two weeks later Cora sat at a table at Mario's, an Italian restaurant in Windsurf, Washington, near her sister Jonna's storm-watching lodge in Coldwater Bay.

This was fine dining at its best. She could hardly believe that she was having dinner with Kirk and they might get a second chance at this. She just hoped she wouldn't mess it up this time.

Her palms were sweaty and her knees trembled. She hated how nervous she felt. She knew Kirk, and it wasn't like it was a first date with him or he wasn't someone she knew well. After all, they'd dated before and then more recently, they'd been through a lot together. A traumatic, dangerous adventure in which they had both almost lost their lives.

All over military secrets and spy stuff. Kirk shared with her that he'd handed off the USB drive containing top secret classified information to his superiors and was commended for his work. But that's all he would say about it. Fine by her. She was just happy to be sitting across from Kirk, an NCIS special agent. No longer working undercover because he didn't want to have to ever lie to her again or to keep secrets.

So sweet.

For her part, she was considering working as a professor at the university so that would keep her closer to home. On occasion, she might take on a shipwreck archaeology project. Kirk had promised her a shipwreck diving trip, just the two of them at some point.

But they had to get through their first dinner date in a long time first.

The lights were dim and a tall candle burned in the middle of a table covered with a white linen tablecloth. Fancy.

Kirk wore a sports jacket over a collared shirt and had used just the right amount of musky cologne. He had made her swoon when he'd picked her up at the inn, but even though he was GQ-cover handsome now, she would miss seeing him dressed in his usual attire on the research vessel—swimming trunks and a T-shirt.

He reached across the table and pressed his hand over hers. Neither of them spoke but it was as if their hearts connected. This was the way it was supposed to have been from the beginning. She wasn't afraid that Kirk would lie to her or afraid of falling in love. She wasn't afraid he wouldn't want her and would discard her when someone better came along. No. They'd both been through too much for her to be concerned that would happen. Their harsh experiences had scraped away all that had kept them apart—past hurts and insecurities.

A man stepped up to the table, pulled a chair out and sat, reminiscent of what Lance and then Commander Jackson had done.

Stephan.

She couldn't believe her eyes. She glanced at Kirk and saw he'd gone pale. Fury boiled behind his gaze. What would he do? Would he act this time? Or just let

Stephan try to sweep her off her feet? She wouldn't go with him, of course, but she needed Kirk to step up and make his claim. Maybe she hadn't gotten over her insecurities, after all.

Stephan took her hand, pulling it out from under Kirk's. He gazed into her eyes. Smiled his charming smile, confident in his ability to win her attention.

"I'm glad you're safe, Cora. I was so worried about you when I heard that the research vessel where you worked had been taken out. It made me realize that I should never have let you go. I love you. I've always loved you. I know I made mistakes, but can you forgive me?"

She glanced at Kirk again, wanting—needing—him to step in and show her that he would fight for her. Then…she remembered the hurt she'd seen in his eyes when a similar scene had played out before and she'd been receptive to Stephan.

Maybe Kirk needed to know what Cora wanted. He had never tried to force her decisions, and right now maybe he wanted to know if Cora would pick him or Stephan this time.

She drew in a calming breath. "You can't be serious. We've been over for a long time, Stephan. Years. I'm here on a date with Kirk, can't you see that?"

Stephan laughed. "I'm a successful attorney, sweetheart. I can take care of you. Buy you things you can only dream about."

"You really are crazy. Have I ever given you the impression that I'm interested in money? You wouldn't know, because you never asked. I'm more interested in someone I can trust. Someone who tells me the truth. Now, please leave."

Kirk stood from his chair and buttoned his sports coat. He stood next to Stephan and grabbed his arm. She hoped there wouldn't be a scene.

"Come on, Stephan. You're not going to do this again. You need to leave."

"Who is going to make me? You?"

He scowled at Stephan. "That's right."

"Sorry, bro. I'm not going anywhere."

"Enough is enough. This behavior is unbecoming to a lawyer from Higgins and Sons." Kirk made to twist Stephan's arm behind his back. "Come on. You had your chance with Cora and you blew it."

Stephan stood and moved quickly away. Threw up his hands in surrender. "Okay, okay. I'm leaving."

Kirk left her to usher Stephan out of the restaurant. Perhaps they had words outside the doors. Cora didn't care. She beamed inside and out.

"You look ravishing." A voice whispered in her ear as warmth tickled her cheek.

Kirk slipped into the seat across from her and smiled. "I apologize for my brother."

"I'm sure we've seen the end to his interference."

"Cora… I need to tell you something."

A measure of fear flitted through her heart. Oh, no. He was going to reject her, after all. "Go ahead."

"I don't want to scare you, but we've been through a lot together, and I want to be up front with you."

"You *are* scaring me."

He gave a nervous laugh, so unlike Kirk. "The first time I saw you, I thought you were the girl for me."

"What do you mean…? You mean, as in marriage?"

He nodded. "I'm telling you this now because if

that's not how you see us, not how you see this going, then maybe this should be our last dinner together."

"What? You're not going to woo me and try to convince me that you're the one for me?"

"I figure that if you don't know by now, you're never going to know." Pain crept over his features before he bowed his head, then lifted his gaze back to her. "My biggest regret in life is the day I let you go. I can hardly believe that I'm sitting here with you now and I have another chance. We have another chance, Cora. You're one of the bravest, strongest people I know, and...I could keep going about all the things I admire about you, but I won't. I'll just say this. I love you, Cora. It's as simple as that."

She couldn't help the broad smile that spread across her face and was rewarded with a genuine smile from Kirk. "I'm so sorry about what happened to keep us apart before, Kirk. I regret that, too, and I'm so grateful that God brought us back together. I don't want to mess this up this time. Because I see us together, Kirk. I want to make this—whatever it is—work. I love you so much, and really, I always have. It's always been you."

He rose from the table and lifted her hand, gently pulled her to her feet, and kissed her deeply and thoroughly.

She'd only thought they'd been on an adventure together, but her adventure with Kirk was just starting, and she could tell already that they were going to have plenty of great stories to tell their children and grandchildren—just like her grandfather had told her.

* * * * *

Dear Reader,

Thank you so much for reading *Distress Signal*. I hope you enjoyed the story! Now that I've written the novel, I can look back and see what it was about—or, at least, that it reflects what's happening in my own life. That's why I hope you connected with the story and Cora. She had a plan for her life, a dream—and that dream came true. She was living the dream, but others interfered with that dream and destroyed the plan. Has that ever happened to you? Basically, life will often throw us curveballs, or as I've said recently regarding my own life—a plot twist. So everything is turned on its head and twisted around.

All I know is that no matter what, God is my rock and I trust in Him through it all. Remember that "A man's heart deviseth his way: but the Lord directeth his steps" (Proverbs 16:9). So we might have made plans, but if we trust in the Lord, He'll make a way for us.

I love to hear from my readers. If you'd like to connect with me, you can find out more at my website: ElizabethGoddard.com.

Many blessings!
Elizabeth Goddard

Get 4 FREE REWARDS!

We'll send you 2 FREE Books plus 2 FREE Mystery Gifts.

Love Inspired® Suspense books feature Christian characters facing challenges to their faith... and lives.

FREE Value Over **$20**

SPECIAL EXCERPT FROM

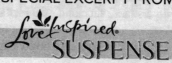

*When her son witnesses a murder, Julia Bradford and
her children must go into witness protection with the
Amish. Can former police officer Abraham King keep
them safe at his Amish farm?*

Read on for a sneak preview of
Amish Safe House by Debby Giusti,
the exciting continuation of the
Amish Witness Protection miniseries,
available February 2019 from Love Inspired Suspense!

"I have your new identities." US marshal Jonathan Mast
sat across the table from Julia in the hotel where she and
her children had been holed up for the last five days.

The Luchadors wanted to kill William so he wouldn't
testify against their leader. As much as Julia didn't trust
law enforcement, she had to rely on the US Marshals and
their witness protection program to keep her family safe.
No wonder her nerves were stretched thin.

"We're ready to transport you and the children,"
Jonathan Mast continued. "We'll fly into Kansas City
tonight, then drive to Topeka and north to Yoder."

"What's in Kansas?"

Jonathan pulled out his phone and accessed a
photograph. He handed the cell to Julia. "Abraham King
will watch over you in Kansas."

Julia studied the picture. The man looked to be in his midthirties with a square face and deep-set eyes beneath dark brows. His nose appeared a bit off center, as if it had been broken. Lips pulled tight and no hint of a smile on his angular face.

"Mr. King doesn't look happy."

Jonathan shrugged. "Law enforcement photos are never flattering."

Her stomach tightened. "He's a cop?"

"Past tense. He left the force three years ago."

Once a cop, always a cop. Her ex had been a police officer. He'd protected others but failed to show that same sense of concern when it came to his own family. The marshal seemed oblivious to her unease.

"Abe is an old friend," Jonathan continued. "A widower from my police-force days who owns a farm and has a spare house on his property. He lives in a rural Amish community."

"Amish?"

"That's right."

"Bonnets and buggies?" she asked.

He smiled weakly. "You'll be off the grid, Mrs. Bradford. No one will look for you there."

Don't miss
Amish Safe House *by Debby Giusti,*
available February 2019 wherever
Love Inspired® Suspense books and ebooks are sold.

www.LoveInspired.com

Looking for inspiration in tales
of hope, faith and heartfelt romance?

Check out **Love Inspired**® and
Love Inspired® **Suspense** books!

New books available every month!

CONNECT WITH US AT:

Facebook.com/groups/HarlequinConnection

Facebook.com/HarlequinBooks

Twitter.com/HarlequinBooks

Instagram.com/HarlequinBooks

Pinterest.com/HarlequinBooks

ReaderService.com

*After returning to his Amish community after losing his
job in the Englisch world, Aaron King isn't sure if he
wants to stay. But the more time he spends training a
horse with childhood friend Sally Stoltzfus, the more he
begins to believe this is exactly where he belongs.*

Read on for a sneak preview of
The Promised Amish Bride *by Marta Perry,
available February 2019 from Love Inspired!*

"Komm now, Aaron. I thought you might be ready to keep your
promise to me."

"Promise?" He looked at her blankly.

"You can't have forgotten. You promised you'd wait until I
grew up and then you'd marry me."

He stared at her, appalled for what seemed like forever until
he saw the laughter in her eyes. "Sally Stoltzfus, you've turned
into a threat to my sanity. What are you trying to do, scare me to
death?"

She gave a gurgle of laughter. "You looked a little bored with
the picnic. I thought I'd wake you up."

"Not bored," he said quickly. "Just…trying to find my way.
So you don't expect me to marry you. Anything else I can do
that's not so permanent?"

"As a matter of fact, there is. I want you to help me train Star."

So that was it. He frowned, trying to think of a way to refuse
that wouldn't hurt her feelings.

"You saw what Star is like," she went on without waiting for
an answer. "I've got to get him trained, and soon. And everyone
knows that you're the best there is with horses."

"I don't think everyone believes any such thing," he retorted.
"They don't know me well enough anymore."

She waved that away. "You've been working with horses

while you were gone. And Zeb always says you were born with the gift."

"Onkel Zeb might be a little bit prejudiced," he said, trying to organize his thoughts. There was no real reason he couldn't help her out, except that it seemed like a commitment, and he didn't intend to tie himself anywhere, not now.

"You can't deny that Star needs help, can you?" Her laughing gaze invited him to share her memory of the previous day.

"He needs help all right, but I don't quite see the point. Can't you use the family buggy when you need it?" He suspected that if he didn't come up with a good reason, he'd find himself working with that flighty gelding.

Her face grew serious suddenly. "As long as I do that, I'm depending on someone else. I want to make my own decisions about when and where I'm going. I'd like to be a bit independent, at least in that. I thought you were the one person who might understand."

That hit him right where he lived. He did understand— that was the trouble. He understood too well, and it made him vulnerable where Sally was concerned. He fumbled for words. "I'd like to help. But I don't know how long I'll be here and—"

"That doesn't matter." Seeing her face change was like watching the sun come out. "I'll take whatever time you can spare. Denke, Aaron. I'm wonderful glad."

He started to say that his words hadn't been a yes, but before he could, Sally had grabbed his hand and every thought flew right out of his head.

It was just like her catching hold of Onkel Zeb's arm, he tried to tell himself. But it didn't work. When she touched him, something seemed to light between them like a spark arcing from one terminal to another. He felt it right down to his toes, and he knew in that instant that he was in trouble.

Don't miss
The Promised Amish Bride *by Marta Perry,*
available February 2019 wherever
Love Inspired® books and ebooks are sold.

www.LoveInspired.com

LIEXP0119